Rescued by a Rake

The Beresford Adventures
Book 4

Cheryl Bolen

© Copyright 2023 by Cheryl Bolen
Text by Cheryl Bolen
Cover by Dar Albert

Dragonblade Publishing, Inc. is an imprint of Kathryn Le Veque Novels, Inc.
P.O. Box 23
Moreno Valley, CA 92556
ceo@dragonbladepublishing.com

Produced in the United States of America

First Edition February 2023
Print Edition

Reproduction of any kind except where it pertains to short quotes in relation to advertising or promotion is strictly prohibited.

All Rights Reserved.

The characters and events portrayed in this book are fictitious. Any similarity to real persons, living or dead, is purely coincidental and not intended by the author.

ARE YOU SIGNED UP FOR DRAGONBLADE'S BLOG?

You'll get the latest news and information on exclusive giveaways, exclusive excerpts, coming releases, sales, free books, cover reveals and more.

Check out our complete list of authors, too!

No spam, no junk. That's a promise!

Sign Up Here

www.dragonbladepublishing.com

⋙⋘

Dearest Reader;

Thank you for your support of a small press. At Dragonblade Publishing, we strive to bring you the highest quality Historical Romance from some of the best authors in the business. Without your support, there is no 'us', so we sincerely hope you adore these stories and find some new favorite authors along the way.

Happy Reading!

Kathryn Le Veque

CEO, Dragonblade Publishing

Additional Dragonblade books by Author Cheryl Bolen

The Beresford Adventures
Lady Mary's Dangerous Encounter (Book 1)
My Lord Protector (Book 2)
With a Little Help from My Lord (Book 3)
Rescued by a Rake (Book 4)

Chapter One

His head hurt like the devil. But Arthur Lansbury, the 4th Earl of Montague—known to his friends as Monty—would not permit the residuals of his profligate nights to interfere with the performance of his daily duties. Even as a lad at Eton, he had never shirked his studies or responsibilities. Not even a bout of lung fever following a frigid swim with his fellow youthful rulebreakers had prevented him from leaving his comforting bed to recite Cicero.

On this early afternoon—for Monty never rose in the morning—he had suffered silently as Cummings shaved him and assisted his master into the clothing he would wear to the House of Lords that day. In addition to Monty's skill as a Corinthian, he was also known to be one of the best dressed men in the Capital.

Before he went to that august chamber, Monty directed his coachman to Half Moon Street. It was well past time he demanded to know why his best friend, the Honorable Thomas Hutchinson, had absented himself from their circle this past week.

It was true Hutch had recently taken the lascivious actress Mrs. Colecott under his protection. Was the blonde Venus so satisfying that Hutch had lost all interest in gathering at Brook's or attending the race meetings at Newmarket?

Even if he had to drag his lifelong friend from his bed, Monty intended to demand an explanation for Hutch's recent reclusiveness. He would also insist that the truant accompany him to Parliament to cast an important vote today on a bill capping the Civil List. The Regent was far too promiscuous with his limitless spending—and this was criticism coming from an earl who spent money rather like one with his own private mint.

Hutchinson's young footman, whose baby face and mop of flaxen hair belied the fellow's six-foot-plus frame, easily recognized Monty, but refrained from swinging the door open wide as he normally did. "I'm afraid my master's not in, Lord Montague."

Monty's brows lowered. It was not yet one in the afternoon. There was no way Hutch would have arisen this morning and already left. His nocturnal habits were in lockstep with Monty's. Neither man ever rose before noon. His friend must not have come home the previous night.

If anyone knew where Hutchinson was, it would be his valet. Hutch was incapable of making himself presentable without the aid of his competent man.

"Might I have a word with Mr. Hutchinson's valet?" Monty asked.

Now the door sprang open, a smile lighting the footman's face. "Certainly, my lord. Should you like to wait in the morning room?"

Monty shook his head as he strode into the mansion's checkerboard entry. "I'll just pop up to Hutch's chambers and save you a trip." With that, the earl began to mount the broad stairway, his gloved hand skimming over the shiny brass banister as generations of Hutchinsons stared down at him from portraits darkened by time.

A moment after Monty entered his friend's bedchamber, the valet opened the door from the adjoining dressing room, a hopeful look on his face. When he saw that Monty was not his master, his expression clouded.

Their eyes locked for a moment. "I was hoping you were Mr. Hutchinson," the man said.

"I take it your employer did not come home last night?"

The middle-aged man morosely shook his head. "Nor for the past week."

Monty could understand how his lusty friend would have no qualms over spending days in the arms of the luscious Mrs. Colecott, but Hutch was far too vain about his appearance to go for a week without the services of his valet. What was the man's name? Oh, yes, he was Jamison.

"I say, Jamison, do you mean to tell me you have not attended to Mr. Hutchinson in a week?"

"That is correct, my lord."

Not what Monty wanted to hear. "Am I also correct in thinking this is highly irregular behavior for your master?"

"Oh, indeed, my lord. Mr. Hutchinson is very particular about his dress."

"Surely he's sent around for a change of clothing?" Though there might not be an urgent need for fresh clothing in the performance of his newfound duties with Mrs. Colecott, surely Hutchinson could not go a whole week without Jamison's ministrations. Mrs. Colecott's hidden talents must be far more extensive than those demonstrated upon the stage of Drury Lane.

The valet's face fell again. "He has not."

How very singular. "Do you know where he's gone?"

Jamison shook his head.

"When was the last time you saw him?"

"Monday last. I believe he was going to meet you and the other young men of your circle at Brook's that night."

That was the last time Monty had seen his friend. Hutch had lost rather heavily at Faro that same night. Monty gave himself a mental shrug. That could explain his friend's need to lose himself in Mrs. Colecott's arms. Once again, Monty's appreciation for the lady's suspected talents increased. She must be exerting considerable influence over his friend.

Granted that after such heavy gaming losses a fellow might need to assuage his sorrow for a time, but Monty could never approve of a man who turned his back on his responsibilities. Even though Monty himself had been elevated to the House of Lords, he kept abreast of important legislation in the House of Commons, where Hutch served. Both men had always been conscientious over their Parliamentary duties, and as in most everything, these boyhood friends shared the same political views.

It wasn't like Hutch to miss an important vote like this one today in the House of Commons. Perhaps he would surprise Monty and show up at Parliament in last week's clothing to cast his vote.

But Monty did not think so. He doubted Mrs. Colecott's abilities extended to shaving a man's face.

⇶⇷

FOR TWO DAYS now Lucy Beresford had been rattling around Devere House on London's Curzon Street with no companionship other than her maid, Hannah. Both her newlywed cousins were guests of the Regent at the Royal Pavilion in Brighton after Harriett and her new husband, Lord Rockingham, foiled a plot to kill His Highness. Every newspaper in the kingdom had written about the events, and Lucy had so looked forward to hearing all the details of her cousin's heroic efforts.

It was actually those two weddings that had precipitated this visit of Lucy's to the Capital. In addition to wanting to meet the new husband of Lucy's favorite cousin, Harriett, Lucy had decided she, too, wanted to join the ranks of the married. It was time to force the hand of the man she'd been promised to since the year of her presentation, some six years ago.

It was time the Honorable Thomas Hutchinson settled down. She meant to ensure that said Reluctant Bridegroom would honor the promise he'd made to her late father, who had already advanced a not-insignificant portion of her significant dowry to her betrothed. Papa had been exceedingly fond of Mr. Hutchinson. Both enjoyed impressive stables, the races at Newmarket, and stiff wagering at the gentlemen's clubs that dotted St. James Street.

Though she had spent years poring over newspaper accounts of her fiancé's escapades, she had in actuality spent very little time with the man with whom she was expected to spend the rest of her life. There were four different occasions when she'd danced with him at Almack's, one Christmas spent with his family and her family—and a host of others—at the Hutchinson's country home in Somerset, and the five-minute private session with him in which he'd begged for her hand in marriage.

She had been so nervous in his presence that day, she'd barely been able to respond to his important question. In physical attributes, the Honorable Thomas Hutchinson was far above her touch. Mr. Hutchinson was uncommonly handsome; Lucy was disappointingly drab.

As alien as it was to her nature, she meant to finally assert herself to her betrothed. Truth be told, she was rather out of charity with him. Not only had he kept her dangling above the shelf for the past six years, but now he had further bruised her pride by ignoring the letter she'd sent around to his house upon her arrival in London.

Two days and still he had failed to call upon his future wife.

She had convinced herself another woman had stolen his affections—not that she was foolish enough to believe she had ever genuinely held his affections. But if it were true that he had bestowed his love on another, Lucy needed to know. Though she fancied herself in love with Mr. Hutchinson, she was well aware that she was also in love with the idea of being married, of being mistress of her own home, of becoming a mother. If Mr. Hutchinson could not oblige her, she would spend this time in London finding another man who would.

Even if such a pursuit went against her reserved nature.

I must be more assertive, she told herself. With that repetitive reinforcement, she donned her bonnet and pelisse and, accompanied by Hannah, began to stroll the short distance from Devere House on Curzon Street to Mr. Hutchinson's house on Half Moon Street. Each step of the way, she coached herself to exert more aggressiveness.

It was an unseasonably warm day for March. Despite the month's ushering in of sturdy, bright-yellow daffodils, it had always seemed to her that March was England's coldest month. Nary a March had come when snow hadn't blanketed her family's Lincolnshire home, Tilford Hall. Today, however, she could have come off without her woolen pelisse.

"I don't like London," Hannah protested.

"But until you came to me, you got along well here in the Capital."

The maid frowned. "That was before you permitted me to read your newspapers. Now I know about all them women what get their throats slashed by madmen."

Lucy stopped in her stride and gazed at her maid. "I may have to withdraw my consent to you reading my newspapers. I know of no one in Mayfair who's met such a gruesome fate as you seem to relish reading about."

Hannah stuck out her lower lip. "Well, I ain't going to Hyde Park."

"Because of that woman who drowned in the Serpentine?"

Hannah nodded sheepishly.

"I believe that was a suicide."

"Slewicide or not, I ain't going."

"*Suicide*. Though I do admit your mispronunciation makes more sense." Lucy sighed. "I had no idea you were such a worrier. You ooze with confidence."

"I have confidence because I'm smart enough to know about dangers and pitfalls."

During her five-minute walk, not a single horse or conveyance passed. This quiet little corner of Mayfair would give first-time visitors to the Capital a false impression of bustling London, the busiest and surely the largest metropolis in the world. The city had always invigorated her. Perhaps this time it would finally erase—or at least stifle—her timidity.

As she neared Hutchinson House, she began to inwardly tremble. Her heartbeat drummed madly. She came to a dead stop and drew in a deep breath, her eyes never leaving the narrow-yet-stately house. *I may soon be mistress here.* She gazed at it appreciatively. Not a particularly large house, its deep red brick with its stark white trim and perfectly symmetric design conveyed a certain restrained elegance. It suddenly occurred to her she had never stepped foot inside what was to be her future home. The very notion of doing so today gave her the mental boost she needed to take those last few steps up to the door.

A moment after her knock, a youthful footman answered. Upon seeing a young woman who was obviously accompanied by her maid, his brows elevated. She knew enough about London customs to know that it was generally not permissible for unmarried ladies to call upon unmarried gentlemen. Such knowledge almost caused her to lose her nerve. And her voice.

But, she told herself, *I am not merely an unmarried lady. I am betrothed to the man who owns this house.* Did that not firmly establish her as something squarely between being a married lady and maiden? Did that not at least give her the right to be there, even without the escort of other genteel companions?

I must be more assertive. "I have come to see the man to whom I am betrothed," she announced.

Now the young footman's brows lowered. "And who might that man be?"

Disappointment bit into her. Even if they had never seen her before, his servants ought to know their master was engaged to be married to the cousin of the Earl of Devere. "Mr. Thomas Hutchinson.

I am Miss Lucy Beresford, calling upon the man I intend to marry, the man who honored me with an offer of marriage."

"Oh." For a moment, the overgrown lad (for the footman had to be considerably younger than she was) stared at her before remembering his customary duties. "Mr. Hutchinson is not in. You're the second one in the past half hour wanting to see my absent master."

She came close to turning away in disappointment, but she fortified herself to demand (in an uncharacteristic manner) who else was calling on the man who was *her* intended. "May I inquire as to who else came to see Mr. Hutchinson today?"

She supposed she must have expressed herself in a forceful way, for the footman answered without hesitation. "Lord Montague."

Lucy did not know Lord Montague, but she knew quite a bit about him. He was Mr. Hutchinson's closest friend and was said to be one of the most scandalous rakes in all of London. At least that is what she had gleaned about him from the snippets of gossip she'd read in the newspapers. She had no desire to be acquainted with such a man.

It came as a surprise to her that Lord Montague would not have known his friend's whereabouts.

She handed the footman her card. "When your master comes home, I beg that you tell him I called. And could I also beg that you remind him of the letter I sent two days ago to notify him that I've arrived in London?"

"It's not likely my master ever received your letter."

"Whyever not?"

"Because my master is away from home."

She forced herself to speak with the authority of one accustomed to being answered. "Where is he?"

The blond footman shrugged his shoulders. "We don't know."

His staff did not know. His best friend did not know. His insignificant fiancée most assuredly did not know.

Her voice reverted to its normal timidness. "Well . . . when you do see Mr. Hutchinson, please see that he gets my letter."

Lucy's spirits were low as they began to walk back to Curzon Street, but Hannah could often be counted upon to coax a chuckle.

"Mrs. Rutherford was tellin' us about young women and girls being snatched away by those in white slavery rings," Hannah said. "If they caught me, I expect I'd be unfortunate enough to be stuck as a scullery maid."

A smile tweaking at her lips, Lucy stopped and turned to her maid. "I believe you may be confused on just the nature of what white slavery is. I assure you, being a scullery maid is far preferrable to what it actually entails."

"I know that slaves have no say in what duties they perform, that they get assigned the most undesirable jobs."

"But when women and girls are abducted by these slavery rings, they're put into . . . brothels—some even in foreign countries, like a sultan's harem."

Hannah gasped. "Oh, miss, you are right! I'd rather work in the scullery from sunup to sundown than to be that sort of slave! Oh, it doesn't bear thinking of! I cringe just thinking about a fat, toothless man trying to take liberties with me. I believe I'd rather die."

"I would, too, but I don't think you need to have any fears. I've not heard of any instances of white slavery gangs in any part of London which we frequent."

They returned to her cousin's lonely house. Why was it when she came to London, all of her loved ones fled? If Harriett were here, she would surely know someone who could discover where Mr. Hutchinson was.

It was really most shocking that Lord Montague had no knowledge of where his friend might be. Though, if she were one inclined to wager, she would bet that by this time tomorrow, the Earl of Montague would have located him. With that in mind, she sat down at the escritoire in her silken turquoise bedchamber and penned a note to the Earl of Montague asking him to call upon her.

Chapter Two

WHO THE DEVIL was Miss Lucy Beresford? And why was the brazen woman writing to him? Monty knew none of Devere's sisters were called Lucy. Such a pity all three of those beauties were now wed. Dare he hope this Lucy was half as lovely as the former Lady Sophia Beresford, who was now married to one of the sinfully wealthy Birminghams?

Monty might as well call around at Devere House today and satisfy his curiosity. He had little else to do. After discovering Hutchinson missing from the House of Commons yesterday, Monty had made inquiries about his friend at White's and Brook's, but no one had seen Hutch.

He stared at the lady's missive. Her hand lacked the flourishes that characterized most women's handwriting. As if written on invisible lines, this woman's script was quite small and exceedingly neat. Even without the flourishes, it was distinctively feminine.

My Dear Lord Montague,

Would you be so kind as to call upon me at Devere House on Curzon at your convenience? I wish to discuss with you an important matter concerning a mutual friend.

Most sincerely,
Lucy Beresford

How could they have a mutual friend when he had no idea who she was? From the surname and the fact that she was staying at Devere House, he deduced she must be a Beresford cousin.

That deduction struck a long-buried memory . . . by Jove! After a nasty string of gaming losses a few years back, Hutch had gotten himself engaged to a Beresford cousin to help cover his debts.

While Monty had never met the chit, he knew two things about her: she had a fat dowry, and she was plain. Which explained why her father had been particularly anxious to marry her off to Hutch.

Now, at least, Monty knew who their mutual friend was. No doubt, Miss Beresford would be trying to locate her missing fiancé. The very thought of Hutchinson's absence sent Monty's gut plummeting. The two men had been friends since the age of seven when they both began at Eton, and in all that time, each of them always knew what the other one was doing. Hutchinson's mysterious disappearance was unprecedented.

Monty felt something was wrong. Dear God, had last week's gaming losses been enough to cause Hutch to do away with himself?

Before Monty called upon the plain Miss Beresford, he would seek out Mrs. Colecott. He prayed that's where Hutch had been this week past.

※※※

MRS. COLECOTT HAD been treading the boards since he and Hutch were barely more than lads entering Oxford. She had enjoyed the favor of many men of noble birth and fat purse. It was said the late Duke of Queensberry, while in his dotage, had settled a fashionable Bayswater Road mansion upon the lovely actress.

It was to that house that Monty had now directed his coachman. As his carriage pulled in front of it, Monty affirmed that the house was, indeed, most fashionable. It was constructed of Portland stone with large, mullioned windows and a shiny black door adorned by a gleaming brass knocker. The off-center door stood proudly at the top a trio of steps.

Monty climbed the steps and knocked.

He waited a moment, but there was no answer. He knocked again. Eventually, an elderly man he presumed to be the butler answered the door, raising a pair of bushy white brows in a haughty manner.

Monty presented his card.

The butler's expression softened when he read the Montague title, and he looked up with something akin to a smile. "My mistress is not in."

"Would I be presumptuous if I were to ask when you expect her to return?"

The other man hesitated a moment before answering. "I couldn't say, my lord. You see, Mrs. Colecott has gone to Bath."

Monty's first reaction was relief that nothing was wrong with Hutchinson. He'd merely gone off to Bath. But then, he knew Hutch well enough to know he would never consider going off like that without Jamison or portmanteaus of his finely tailored clothing.

"I don't mean to pry, but I believe the lady is acquainted with Mr. Hutchinson, who is my closest friend. Could you tell me if he accompanied her to Bath?"

"I believe it was he who sent a note to Mrs. Colecott, asking her to meet him in Bath."

Relief rushed over him as he thanked the butler and took his leave. At least Hutch hadn't put an end to his own life!

But something was still wrong. Monty did not believe Hutch would have gone to Bath without his valet. He decided to make one more stop before calling on Miss Beresford and returned to Half Moon Street. Hutch's young footman immediately recognized him. "Good afternoon, Lord Montague."

With the air of one who owned the house, Monty stepped into the foyer. "I've come to see if Mr. Hutchinson may have left a message." He proceeded to Hutchinson's library. The walls of the library were lined with dark wooden shelves crammed with leather books. Dark wood extended to the chamber's large writing table.

He supposed the owner's long absence accounted for the fact the scarlet silken draperies had not been opened. Monty walked to the tall Italianate casement and drew open the drapes in order to see better. Then he went to the untidy writing table where piles of papers and last week's periodicals were stacked. Just between two stacks, he spotted a slip of paper. The handwriting bore a striking resemblance to Hutch's. His stomach turned when he read the words.

I know what I have to do.

Good lord, could Hutch actually have been contemplating suicide? Was it too late to stop him? If only he knew where his friend was.

If he was still alive.

With a grievously heavy heart, Monty left the house and instructed his coachman to Curzon Street, though he probably could have walked the short distance in equal time.

⫸⫷

LUCY HAD NOT left Devere House that day. She would not miss seeing Lord Montague when he called. It wasn't as if she actually wanted anything to do with the lecherous man. If half the accounts of him she had read in the newspapers were true, he was a most disreputable person. Of course, her own affianced was reputed to be just as wicked, but her dear, slightly unconventional papa had handpicked the man to be her husband. Her papa had his faults, but she could never deny that he adored her—his eldest daughter—above all others, and he only ever wanted what he thought was best for her.

Buried in Lincolnshire, she had little opportunity to mingle with peers of the realm, so it was important to her now that she wear her most fashionable dress to greet his lordship. She couldn't have him thinking his handsome friend had the misfortune to be affianced to a clueless spinster from the provinces. Even if that might be an apt description of her.

"Ain't that dress mighty fancy to wear just sitting around yer cousin's house?" Hannah asked. Hannah wasn't like other, demure lady's maids. She was as different from the refined French maids as a donkey was from a thoroughbred. In spite of her rough edges, though, Hannah was possessed of an excellent eye for fashion and was uncommonly talented at styling hair. She was also brutally honest.

What a pity that even the most talented stylist could not render Lucy's whitish blonde locks more alluring.

"If you must know," Lucy said, "I am expecting the Earl of Montague to call today."

Hannah's mossy eyes opened wide. "And what will yer Mr. Hutchinson think about that?"

"The earl is Mr. Hutchinson's closest friend."

"Ah, so you mean to find out where that rascal you're betrothed to is!"

"Indeed I do. I've become most impatient with the man I'm supposed to marry."

Hannah's eyes widened. "You're not going to break it off with him?"

"I don't know. I am going to give him an ultimatum. Then we shall see."

"Pray, what's an ultmatey?"

"*Ultimatum.* It means I'm going to make him choose between his freedom and me."

"It's about time!"

"If Reluctant Bridegroom doesn't want to marry me, I shall find someone else."

Hannah pursed her lips as she slipped a pin into Lucy's hair and stood back to survey her artistry. "Methinks yer papa found someone for you because he knows how shy you are. Do you think yer even capable of flirting?"

Lucy did not answer for a moment. "I hope I don't have to."

"So you still want to marry your Mr. Hutchinson?"

"Of course."

"If he don't want you no more, wouldn't it be nice is his lordly friend took a fancy to you? Of course, you probably ain't pretty enough for an earl."

Even her doting papa had realized Lucy wasn't pretty enough for an earl. She had come to accept her lack of beauty as stoically as she'd come to accept she would be marrying a man who was not in love with her.

Hannah continued. "Still, I fancy myself being maid to a ladyship—not that I'd ever be happy with anyone 'cept you."

"Even with your shamefully truthful tongue, I wouldn't have anyone except you, my dear, brutal Hannah."

The Devere footman rapped at Lucy's bedchamber door. "A Lord Montague is calling on you, Miss Beresford."

She turned to Hannah, suddenly terrified at the prospect of sitting in the same room with a noted rake. If only her cousin Devere were here. "I mustn't see him unchaperoned. Grab that *Ackermann's* and come sit and peruse it whilst I meet him in the drawing room."

"I never heard of pursuing a magazine."

"*Peruse.* Not pursue." Lucy rolled her eyes and explained, "Peruse simply means to look it over."

"Why didn't you just say that? You and yer fancy words."

Lucy stood up and peered into the looking glass. The lavender dress with puffy little lace-trimmed sleeves and an elegant drape of sarcenet was lovely. Her hair, fashioned in a Grecian mode, was elegant. But the skinny lady herself was sadly wanting in beauty.

Clutching the newest edition of *Ackermann's,* Hannah followed her mistress down the staircase. When they entered the drawing room, a slumped-over Hannah went straight to the far corner to scan the magazine, where she would be little noticed, little noticing, and largely out of earshot, while Lord Montague stood and greeted Lucy by bending and brushing his lips over her gloved hand. "It's a pleasure to finally meet Hutchinson's fiancée."

She did not know what she expected, but this man was not it. If possible, he was even more handsome than Mr. Hutchinson. He was taller than his friend and appeared to display the same exceptional fashion sense that Mr. Hutchinson did.

She supposed because of his reputation she must have expected him to be sporting a pair of horns. Therefore, she was unprepared for the perfection of his manly face. Excellently cut dark hair spilled onto his forehead, its color a perfect match to his eyes that were as dark as rich coffee beans.

There was strength in his pensive face, aristocratic breeding in his aquiline nose, and a touch of playfulness about his mouth that rose above a clefted, dimpled chin. The man stole her breath away.

She dipped into a slight curtsey and nodded. It was a moment before she could respond to his welcome greeting. At least he must know who she was. She had feared that Mr. Hutchinson had never spoken of her even to his closest friend. "Thank you so much, my lord, for coming. Won't you please take a seat?"

He sat at one of a pair of sofas that faced each other near the fireplace. She sat opposite. It went against her nature to initiate a conversation with a gentleman, but as hostess here, she must. It was really most humiliating to admit she had no knowledge of the man to whom she was to plight her troth. "I understand you are the closest friend to Mr. Hutchinson," she began.

"Indeed. It has always been so."

Yet Mr. Hutchinson never saw fit to introduce his dearest friend to his fiancée. Was she nothing more than an insignificant footnote in his life? "I arrived in London three days ago but have not been able to see Mr. Hutchinson. It's rather important that I do. I even went to his house, as I understand you also did, but he wasn't there. I thought by now you might have discovered his whereabouts."

The sublimely handsome Lord Montague drew in a breath, then frowned. "I wish to God I did know with certainty where he is. I haven't seen him in better than a week."

Her face fell.

"Just today I learned that he may be in Bath," he continued, "but I have my doubts as to the veracity of that claim."

All trace of her bashfulness fled. "Why?"

Their eyes locked. Just being stared at by a man of Lord Montague's extreme handsomeness caused her to tremble. Her lashes lowered. It was obvious he did not want to answer her question.

※

IT TOOK MONTY several moments to form a response. Just because he was worried sick about his friend did not give him the right to upset this poor country miss who was pledged to Hutchinson. What if she started to bawl? He could never bear to see a woman cry.

Upon first seeing Miss Lucy Beresford, he thought her one of the most insignificant-looking young women he'd ever met. It was difficult to believe she was cousin to the stunning Sophia Beresford—or Mary or Harriett Beresford. It was even more shocking that Hutch would have consented to marry this chit. Hutch had a long history with beauties. Mrs. Colecott, even though she was a decade older than they were, was still a remarkable beauty.

He'd been thinking of Miss Beresford as a spinster. After all, if he recalled correctly, she had come out some half a dozen years earlier—which would make her at least four-and-twenty.

A frailty about her, though, made her look more like a girl than the mature woman he'd expected. Her skin was so pale he could easily picture her reclined on a chaise while last rites were being administered.

Adding to her fragile aura was the slenderness of her delicate body. Did the lady never eat?

Monty tried to determine why Miss Beresford's appearance did not satisfy. There was nothing unobjectionable in her appearance. It was just that it was . . . plain.

At least she dressed well, and her hair was styled in the latest fashion.

But when his eyes locked with hers, he had to admit she was possessed of very fine eyes. They were larger than average and an exquisite shade of blue, rather like the sky on a bright, summer day.

The lady's obvious discomfort in social intercourse indicated she was reticent. In every way, she was in opposition to every female who had ever caught Hutch's eye.

How could Monty answer her question? He could not very well tell a maiden that her betrothed was the protector of the notorious Mrs. Colecott. He must skirt the truth to the best of his ability. He cleared his throat. "I called at the house of a . . . friend of Mr. Hutchinson's." He would not lie, but he had no qualms about omitting some of the truth. "The friend was not in but had gone to Bath, so said the footman. According to the servant, Hutch requested via a note this person's presence in Bath." He paused. "I am not convinced my friend sent the letter."

"Why?" Even her voice was thin.

"Because Mr. Hutchinson would never go out of town without his valet and clothing." He frowned. "His valet hasn't seen him since the last day I was with him. Night actually."

She nodded knowingly. "And that was at least a week ago?"

"Yes."

"And I take it he's collected no clothing, either?"

"Correct."

Her gaze shifted to the window which looked out over the street in front of the house. She swallowed. "Your reluctance to use a pronoun in connection with the friend who's now in Bath tells me that friend is a female."

Miss Beresford might lack experience in the *ton*, but she made up for that void with a solid understanding of the *ton's* ways. His first inclination was to lie, but to lie to this forthright woman would not be right. Besides, he abhorred lying.

Yet he could hardly acknowledge Hutch's connection to the actress. A murky response was called for. "Be assured, theirs is not a relationship which would interfere with nuptials between you and my friend."

Her lashes lowered as deep red climbed into her cheeks.

She realizes Hutch has a ladybird.

A silence like that in the darkness before dawn filled the chamber.

After several moments, she spoke. "So where do you think your friend is?"

He shrugged. "To be honest, I have ruled out all the places where I thought he might be."

"And after that, do you have any guesses?"

How could he tell her he feared his friend had committed suicide? Yet . . . perhaps he should be preparing her for the possibility that she might never see Hutch again. "I've asked myself that a hundred times."

"I will own, my lord, it is most perplexing—even horrifying."

As upset as he was over Hutch, he took an odd, perverse comfort in being able to share this worry with someone else. "Most alarming."

She nodded, her well-coiffed head moving almost unperceptively. Then as she began to speak, her voice shook. "It sounds as if Mr. Hutchinson may have met with foul play."

He shut his eyes tightly. She must be stronger than he, for he could not give voice to such fears. "There is one more thing."

Her pale brown eyebrows rose.

"That last night . . ."

Her eyes met his, and there was an unmistakable look of anguish in them. "Go on," she managed in a trembling voice.

"He was gaming and lost heavily."

Neither spoke for a moment. She was no fool. His unsaid words were etched in her expression.

He might have taken his own life.

"And there's something else," he finally added, drawing in a shaky breath. "I found a note on his desk. Quite a distressing note."

Her frightened eyes met his. "A note in Mr. Hutchinson's hand?"

"I believe so."

"What did it say?"

"It was a single line. *I know what I have to do.* I am not sure what it means. Though it is possible it has something to do with the duties he performs at the Foreign Office."

"I didn't even know he served at the Foreign Office."

"I doubt he does anything very important. He has always claimed he just pushes around papers."

She said nothing for a moment. "I can tell you're most distressed, my lord. You fear for your friend's life, do you not?"

She had to be as distraught as he, yet she seemed more concerned about his feelings. He merely nodded. Normally, he did not admit to anything as emasculating as harboring fears, but he felt almost relieved to be able to share these numbing fears with another.

"Then I suggest we satisfy our curiosity by elimination."

Her timidness had vanished like the snuffing of a candle. "How do you propose to do that?" he asked.

"We must go to Bath."

Chapter Three

For a moment he was too stunned to speak. Was this woman in want of a brain? "We?" he asked, incredulous.

"On the chance that my betrothed *is* there, I can consent to a hasty marriage that would allow him to settle all his debts. I just might be the instrument of saving his life."

He had to admit, that could be a solution to his friend's problems. *If he's still alive.* But it was most improper. "I am aware you've spent most of your life . . ." Where in the devil had she lived? That damned Hutch never spoke to him of the poor woman. ". . . in the country. Are you aware that an unmarried lady is not permitted to travel with a man who is not her husband—especially on a journey which will necessitate spending a night at an inn?"

She straightened her spine and glared at him. "Of course I am aware of that! But it's not as if . . ." She clamped shut her mouth. Color hiked into her pale cheeks.

He finished her thought. *As if she would be offering herself for seduction.* Apparently, the very notion of being seduced embarrassed her. He felt beastly that he was the cause of her distress.

"Will one of your parents accompany us?" Why had he gone and spoken as if he were consenting to her foolish plan?

Her lashes lowered. "Both my parents are dead."

"I'm sorry." His voice changed from somber to hopeful when he added, "I say, is James Beresford your brother?"

"Indeed he is. My eldest brother. Do you know him?"

He nodded. "Devere introduced us at Brook's one night. Your brother is head of your branch of the family now?"

"Yes. He's become rather enamored of agricultural improvements and has directed all of his attentions to improving the production of our lands in Lincolnshire."

"How many acres?"

She shrugged. "I daresay about one hundred thousand."

No wonder those Beresford pockets were so deep. But overseeing such an estate meant that James Beresford was too far away to chaperone any journey to Bath. "Then who would you propose to serve as chaperone?"

"My maid."

He could think of nothing more constricting than traveling over one hundred miles with a lady's maid as a companion. Furthermore, he saw no reason why Miss Beresford should feel compelled to accompany him at all. If a hasty marriage was indeed necessary, he could get Hutch back to London on his own quickly enough "I cannot be a part of this scheme of yours."

"Tell me this, my lord: Were you considering making a trip to Bath?"

"It had crossed my mind."

"I understand your desire to exhaust all avenues to find your friend. Please try to understand mine."

"Why can you not simply go to Bath on your own without me traveling with you?" he asked.

"I am not permitted to ride in public conveyances like the mail coach. My brother sent me to London in our family carriage, but it's now returned to Lincolnshire."

"Then you propose to ride with me in my coach?"

She nodded shyly.

"Are you aware of my reputation?"

More crimson crept into her cheeks as she managed a slight nod.

"Your good name would be ruined if anyone witnessed you with me under such circumstances, with or without your maid."

"I don't give a fiddle for my good name when Mr. Hutchinson's very life is at stake."

She obviously cared far more for Hutch than he cared for her.

"Then allow me to offer the usage of my coach. I will stay in London and continue to look for Hutchinson."

She glared. "I know I said I care not for my good name, but you surely can't expect me to present myself at the residence of my affianced's ladybird?"

Now it was difficult for him to look her in the eye. This was far too delicate a matter to be discussing with a maiden, an unmarried lady of good birth.

Of course Miss Beresford could not be permitted to come face-to-face with Mrs. Colecott. She ought not to even learn the name of the infamous actress in connection with Hutch.

As deeply as he cared for his friend, at this moment Monty was cursing Hutchinson for putting him in such a perplexing position. And for petrifying him with worry.

He had to admit, the lady had a point. That task of speaking with the actress should fall squarely upon his own shoulders. "Of course not. In that case, I see no need for you to come. I'll go to Bath by myself. I promise to keep you apprised of what I learn."

She shook her head. "It is not for you to concern yourself with my reputation, my lord. I am of age, and I must insist upon going to Bath. Now that you have acquainted me with the potential danger to Reluctant Bridegroom, I shall be prostate with worry until I learn his fate. The sooner, the better."

He had been taken aback for a moment when she referred to Hutchinson as Reluctant Bridegroom. Then, he'd almost guffawed over how accurately it described Hutch. Monty looked into her extraordinary eyes. And thought of their traveling alone and how it could tarnish her. "Do you believe yourself capable of fending off advances from a lecher like me?" Even though heretofore this had been a morose conversation, now it was all he could do not to laugh. Monty had never been interested in seducing plain women.

She refused to look him in the eye when she responded. "I choose to believe you will behave in a gentlemanly fashion."

He turned somber. "I give you my word, I will."

HAD LORD MONTAGUE just consented to her plan? She could almost feel her chest swelling with pride. For in those hours leading up to his lordship's visit, she had instructed herself to *be assertive*. Exerting herself like that may have been the most difficult thing she'd ever done. (Except for the time she'd had to undress her inebriated brother and tuck him into bed before their stern papa found him sprawled on the stairs.)

She was still somewhat dazed by her ability to project a degree of authority. More than once, she had managed to stop herself from conceding to Lord Montague. When he told her to stay in London, she had started to nod her capitulation. When he'd said for her to go on to Bath alone, she had almost consented, but then her newly discovered defiance raised its head and had its way.

Even when he'd practically threatened to seduce her, she had brazenly called his bluff. From whence had this new-found boldness come? Would the usually reticent Miss Lucy Beresford be able to maintain this new persona?

Though now, as the handsome earl met her gaze and spoke so earnestly, she felt as if she were melting inside. Before meeting him, she had been terrified at the thought of coming face to face with such a profligate. Now that he'd pledged to respect her, she was possessed of the feeling that he was sincere. She was convinced his pledge had more to do with her lack of appeal than his abundance of honor. Nevertheless, she believed him.

I must convey maturity. She looked him squarely in the eye and spoke with a confidence she was far from feeling. "When do we leave?"

He merely stared at the floor. No expression showed in his face, save for a tightening vein in his throat.

As the seconds ticked away, her heartbeat began to drum. He was going to change his mind—she could feel it. She would not be permitted to go with him. She felt like a nag whose Tattersall's auction drew no bidders.

Finally those dark eyes of his lifted, his gaze meeting hers. "Would that your brother were here in London to lend propriety."

"My brother won't be coming to the Capital any time in the near future." She frowned. "He's always been possessed of an obsessive personality. When he first left Oxford, he was passionate about gambling. Whist, Faro, any wager that relied on chance demanded his full attention, seven days and seven nights a week. Then he went through a phase where he was horse mad. He spent at least two years immersed in horse breeding and race meetings to the exclusion of all else. Then last year, he turned his full attention to agriculture. There is no book on animal husbandry or modern farming methods he hasn't read. I must say, this newest obsession of his has been the only one which has increased his wealth—which I suppose bodes well for future generations of Beresfords."

He nodded thoughtfully as his attention returned to the Axminster carpet. "He seemed a nice fellow. I shouldn't wish for him to call me out. Pistols at dawn, and all that, you know."

"James wouldn't do that. He abhors violence. He doesn't even condone pugilism."

"That's reassuring. I shouldn't want to harm him, either."

"You mustn't worry about my brother's objections. He'll not learn of my indiscretion in traveling to Bath with you. We'll not tell anyone."

"But it's possible we'd be seen."

"It's not likely that someone of my acquaintance would be at a coaching inn between London and Bath, an inn where we would take separate chambers. I know very few people outside of my village in Ambelbury. I had just the one not-very-successful Season. And you cannot deny that my appearance is not likely to burn an indelible impression in anyone's mind, either. I'm quite ordinary looking."

He did not attempt to refute her statement. While approving of his innate honesty, she was disappointed. It wasn't that she would ever expect him to find her appearance out of the ordinary. Her disappointment stemmed from her lack of beauty. How fortunate were those ladies whose loveliness drew admirers.

"Before my brother could even learn of my unauthorized jaunt, I hope to be a married woman. I assure you, that would make my brother very happy. You see, he has three more sisters to launch, and he has vowed not to do so until I wed." She shrugged. "James is a most tolerant brother, but my sisters can be most vexing. His life will be much more enjoyable when I'm married, and I can see to our sisters' presentations."

"But what if . . ."

"If Mr. Hutchinson's not in Bath?"

He did not answer. The solemn look on his sun-burnished face and the way he'd not been able to finish his sentence told her the earl was even more troubled than she'd first thought over the possibility his friend had taken his own life. Finally, he nodded.

He stood and began to pace the chamber, deep in thought. She was stuck by the fine quality of his clothing. Her cousin Devere had heretofore been her arbiter of male fashion. And the few times she'd seen her betrothed, she had admired his taste in clothing. Had he been influenced by Lord Montague?

He stopped in front of the stone-cold fireplace and addressed her. "My coach will come here at dawn. You will be permitted to bring your maid. She'll ride in a hired conveyance with my valet. I don't want her or my man to know about Hutch. You and I will be free to discuss the situation in the privacy of my coach. I will ask that you travel light. I'll not have towers of portmanteaus and valises on top of my coach slowing us down."

Lord Montague was going to permit her to accompany him to Bath! Now she glowed like the nag who'd been selected to convey the king. She was too pleased that her plan was going forward to be out of charity with his lordship's didactic manner. Inheriting a title affected many aspects of one's life. Like taking one's seat in the House of Lords, acquiring a grand country home, and adopting an authoritarian manner.

Were Lord Montague her brother, she would have rushed and thrown her arms around him. But he was not James. Or even her younger brother, Chuckie, for that matter. He was an earl. A very handsome earl who was most assuredly one of the most sought-after lords in all the kingdom. What beauty would not wish to capture this man's heart?

Restrain yourself. "Thank you, my lord. I will be ready at dawn, and I'll bring just one valise. Will that be agreeable to you?"

"It will." He moved toward the door, then turned back and sketched a bow. "Until tomorrow, Miss Beresford."

<hr />

AFTER DIRECTING HIS coachman to Westminster, Monty settled back in his carriage, shaking his head. How in the devil had he gotten himself locked into a journey with a respectable maiden? He was not looking forward to it, but it was vital that he learn his best friend's fate.

He sighed. Today's session at the House of Lords promised to last through the night. He would not stay the full time. He had to rise exceedingly early—something he was unaccustomed to doing. He dreaded the long, dull trip with Devere's dull cousin.

But there was nothing he wouldn't do for Hutch.

Chapter Four

Lucy had been so focused on finding her missing betrothed, she had not considered her propensity to suffer from carriage sickness. How humiliated she would be to cast up her accounts in front of the dashing earl. She would do anything in her power to avoid such embarrassment. If she did not eat, she reasoned, surely there would be nothing to expel. Therefore, she had declined dinner the previous night and had not consumed a morsel this morning.

She stood in the darkened foyer of Devere House just before the sun rose. She dared not alienate his lordship by not being ready when he arrived. She knew enough of the ways of the *ton* to be aware that gentlemen of his class never rose early in the day. That he was willing to do so indicated just how worried he was about his best friend.

As was she.

"I am glad we don't have to walk these streets in the dark," Hannah said. "I keep remembering about that woman what got stabbed three-and-forty times. I ask you, why would someone plunge a knife that many times? I should think it would only take one or two tries to get the same result. Unless the murderer was a madman. Which I suppose he was."

Hannah was unduly fascinated by tales of gory crimes, just the kind of newspaper accounts Lucy had no interest in reading.

Lord Montague's crested coach, illuminated by carriage lanterns, came into view. To save him from having to climb the steps and rap at her door, Lucy and Hannah, each dragging a valise, immediately darted from the house.

His coachman leapt from the box and came around to open the carriage door, let down the steps, and take her bag while Hannah went to the smaller vehicle behind his lordship's grand coach.

Inside the Montague carriage, the earl greeted her. "I pray, Miss Beresford, you are in better spirits this morning than I."

Though the light was not yet good, she settled into her seat across from him and took a long look at the earl. She had expected him to demonstrate the ravages of a late night of sottishness. Is that not what these London men did? But he did not appear to be suffering the effects of the dissipation she had previously associated with him. He actually looked well rested.

And bored.

She was so grateful to him for allowing her as his traveling companion, she wanted to say, "I will be in whatever spirits you wish me to be, my lord," but she decided against fawning over the mighty peer. It was best she comport herself as one with aristocratic lineage, not as a country miss agog with peer worship. Though she held no Honorable or Lady in front of her name, her grandfather had been the Earl of Devere, a title currently held by her cousin, who had inherited from her uncle—her father's brother.

She spoke only barely above a whisper. "I actually feel guilty for so thoroughly looking forward to going to Bath, which I know I should not be feeling under these grave circumstances."

"You've been to Bath before?"

She shook her head. "Never."

"Then it is a pity so worrisome a situation will bring us to the city. In spite of the many invalids who flock there for its waters, Bath can be a lively place. The assemblies are most popular. I believe you'll be impressed with the uniformity of architecture in the classical style. It's an aesthetically pleasing city surrounded by green hills."

He did not speak like a lecher—not that she actually knew how lechers spoke. She wasn't precisely sure if she'd ever been in the presence of one. She would own, though, that most rakes did not give a fiddle about the aesthetics of a city. Her cousin Sophia Beresford, now Sophia Birmingham—who had turned down seven-and-forty proposals of marriage and knew a great deal about rakes of the *ton*—had told her that all rakes cared about was gaming and fornicating.

Lucy approved of neither.

But she did approve of classical architecture. Very much. How could he possibly have known that?

"I've read about the father and son who built Bath and have admired their work—what I saw of it in paintings."

He nodded. "John Wood the Elder. His son carried out the remainder of his designs after he died."

"And all the buildings are truly constructed of golden-colored stone?"

"Bath stone," he said with a nod.

"I should love to see the Royal Crescent. In the pictures, it looks so very regal."

"You will stay at my house there."

Her eyes widened. "You have a house on the Royal Crescent?"

He nodded. "My father bought it."

"But I couldn't possibly stay at your house." Had he not been the one who was so concerned about her reputation? She would be ruined if she stayed at the bachelor's house without a proper chaperone.

"You will. I'll secure lodgings at a hotel." He had once again adopted his authoritarian tone, and she was incapable of arguing with him.

Even though few vehicles traversed sprawling London at this hour, it still took over an hour to put the city behind them, owing to the abundance of tolls that had to be paid. When they finally reached the country lanes, the sun favored them. Everywhere she looked brought evidence of spring's great greening. Tufts of green sprang up in winter's straw-like grass. Verdant leaves were beginning to flare on barren tree limbs. Blankets of daffodils raised their cheerful heads throughout the countryside and on the perimeter of the cottages scattered along the byway.

What was turning out to be a lovely spring day would have been more enjoyable if her stomach weren't so blasted queasy. Traveling on the city's well-paved streets had no ill effects upon her sensitive stomach, but once they hit the rutted, uneven country lanes she was forced to spend a great deal of time with her eyes shut tightly as she willed her stomach not to betray her.

"Bad luck that you had to come to London when your cousins are away," he said by way of initiating a conversation.

Lucy had rushed to London upon learning of Harriett's hasty marriage, hoping to meet the well-respected member of Parliament her cousin had wed. How was she to know they'd been offered use of the regent's Royal Pavilion at Brighton for their honeymoon—and this just after Devere had married and taken his bride to his ancestral home. "Indeed."

Lucy's one-word responses would never foster a friendly dialogue with Lord Montague. She thought of Harriett. If only she could be more like her popular cousin.

"Have you met Lord Rockingham?" he asked.

"No." Then, cognizant of her inability to converse with a well-heeled Londoner, she forced herself to add, "That is why I wanted to come to London. I'm closest to Lady Harriett and wished to satisfy myself of his worthiness."

"The man is most worthy. I would have been ecstatic if one of my own sisters married a man of Rockingham's many stellar attributes."

"That is most reassuring."

His brows lowered, and he gave her a penetrating gaze. "That cannot be your sole reason for traveling to London, can it?"

Was he baiting her? He must wish to hear about her relationship with Mr. Hutchinson. It was difficult to discuss her fiancé when the man sitting across the carriage from her knew her intended far better than she.

She took a deep breath. Even though speaking of Mr. Hutchinson would expose her to potential humiliation, she felt she owed it to Lord Montague to be honest. After all, he was giving up his beautiful house on the Royal Crescent for her. "There was another reason." She paused. "As you may know, I've been betrothed to Mr. Hutchinson for six years."

He nodded.

"I had decided that I would offer him the opportunity to extricate himself from the engagement if he had changed his mind about marrying me. I have wasted too much time waiting for Reluctant Bridegroom."

He smiled. "So, if you can't marry Hutch, you're determined to marry another?"

"Exactly, my lord." Being married to a penniless country curate was far preferrable to waiting for a handsome gentleman-about-town who had no intention of even being a faithful husband.

"Do you have someone in mind?"

"Not at all. Lest you forget, I've been buried in rural Lincolnshire."

"Then I hope we find him in Bath, and you'll be able to speedily become a married woman. That is, if that's what you and Hutchinson want."

She wanted to ask him if Mr. Hutchinson ever spoke of her, but she was too embarrassed to do so. It was entirely possible her fiancé's discussions of her could have been unflattering. She was aware that Mr. Hutchinson, a handsome, well-connected man, had a history with beautiful women. And she most certainly was *not* a beautiful woman. She prayed he had not ridiculed her.

"I hope so, too," she whispered, then returned her attention to looking out the window.

Five minutes later, he resumed the conversation. "It sounds to me as if you're ready to cry off the betrothal."

She allowed herself a moment to formulate her response. "It's difficult to say. You see, I was torn. On the one hand, my dear papa had selected Mr. Hutchinson. I know Papa had my best interest at heart, and I always endeavored to please my parent. But, you must own, you being Mr. Hutchinson's closest friend, that Mr. Hutchinson does not appear eager to marry me." Even that admission caused her cheeks to burn.

"If that should be the case, you mustn't take it as a personal affront. Hutch just enjoys his freedom. He may have equated marriage with a complete restriction of the activities that brought him pleasure."

"One would think at thirty years of age, one would be more mature, more inclined to set down roots." She could not believe she'd been so forthright with the earl. She had actually criticized his friend. She immediately wished she could take back her words!

He grinned. It was a devastating grin, one that caused her heartbeat to quicken.

"Nine-and-twenty," he corrected.

So she was wrong about Mr. Hutchinson's age.

"I, on the other hand, reached the grand old age of thirty last month."

"Such an old man," she teased, relieved at his good humor.

"Perhaps next month, when Hutch leaves his twenties behind, he will be more inclined to, as you put it, *set down roots*."

Since Lord Montague was being awfully nice to her, she thought to adopt his playful attitude. "Then, my lord, are you ready to set down roots now that you've reached so advanced an age?"

He tossed back his head and chuckled. "Not at present." He

shrugged. "I daresay I just haven't yet met the right woman."

What kind of woman would tame this rake? She would be beautiful. And she would hail from an aristocratic family. A man with his many attributes could merit a duke's daughter.

She almost quipped that he would have an easier time finding a suitable bride if he looked for respectable women. From what she had read of him in the newspapers these past six years, he had liaisons with married ladies, opera dancers, and actresses. But never with a respectable maiden. But it was not her place to chide him, even in jest, especially after he had been so obliging toward her.

At noon, they stopped to stretch their legs and partake of a luncheon. She could have sung her gratitude to the heavens. Now her unsettled stomach could calm—though she certainly had no plans to swallow a morsel of food.

Lord Montague carried the basket up the slope of a small hill. Not a single house or structure was in sight. She helped him spread out the rug at the crest of the hill, and they sat on it. He emptied the contents of the basket: a flask of wine, a loaf of bread, and a block of cheese.

She dared not eat. Would he even notice her abstinence? After all, she must be an insignificant entity to him.

He broke the loaf in half and handed one piece to her.

She shook her head.

His brows lowered. "Then allow me to offer you cheese."

"No, thank you."

His lazy gaze raked over her.

Had he stripped off her clothing, she could not have felt more embarrassed.

"So denying yourself sustenance is what's keeping you so slender?"

No woman wanted to hear that she was skinny. She harrumphed. "Quite the opposite, my lord. I am always eating in the hopes of adding womanly curvature." Her face flamed. She could not believe she had just confessed her humiliating deficiencies to this man who—

except for his profligate reputation—was perfection. Her lids lowered.

Once more, she felt the sweep of his gaze. "There's nothing wrong with being slender, Miss Beresford. Some men prefer it. And have you not noticed that it's the thin women who age much more gracefully? They tend to avoid those sagging body parts."

She broke into laughter. The mention of *sagging body parts* had her envisioning flabby arms weighted down and huge cushions of fat draping from one's midsection.

"What's so funny?"

Their laughing eyes met and held. "*Sagging body parts.* I've never heard anyone speak of such before."

He laughed, too. "It does conjure a comic image." He bit into his crusty bread.

A moment later he asked, "So you don't care for bread?"

"I normally eat bread every day."

"Then?"

She sighed. "I confess I am unable to eat whilst traveling in a carriage."

"Ah ha! So you're a bad sailor?"

It did rather feel like being seasick. "Wretchedly so."

"You cannot go two days without eating."

"I shall try my best to do so."

"You poor girl."

It had been a long while since anyone had referred to her as a girl.

She watched as he ate. If someone had told her a week ago she would be traveling across England alone with this man who was notorious for his prurient ways, she would have been terrified.

Now, though, she found nothing terrifying about him. He could not have treated her in a more gentlemanly fashion. Of course, it would likely have been an altogether different predicament were she a beauty.

Long ago she had come to accept she would never be a beauty as were her Beresford cousins. But in the presence of this gentleman, for reasons she could not entirely comprehend, today she fervently wished she were a beauty.

"Perhaps, Miss Beresford, you should sit a bit more in the shade of the tree. It wouldn't do to burn that fair skin of yours."

Perhaps the fairness of her skin was an attribute. Did not all women aspire to having skin as pale as a bowl of milk? His lordship must have noticed her flesh when he so blatantly perused her from the top of her head to the tips of her slippers minutes earlier.

She scooted back a foot, so close to the tree trunk she could have rested her spine against it.

"When is the last time you ate?" he asked, his voice softening with concern.

"This time yesterday."

"You must try to eat something."

She shook her head adamantly.

"I'm sorry for you."

No woman wished to be considered pitiable by a handsome man. Her face collapsed.

"Because of your affliction," he added. "It must be beastly. I feel like an ogre eating in front of you."

He was much kinder than she had expected. In fact, everything in his demeanor was unexpectedly favorable. She was the one who felt like an ogre for doubting his decency.

"There is nothing in your behavior today that is ogre-ish."

"I did give you my word I would be on my best behavior."

"And you always keep your word?"

"I have many faults, but dishonesty's not one of them." He poured wine into a glass. "Can't you at least join me in drinking a glass of wine?"

"Thank you, but I cannot."

His dark eyes met hers. The solid planes of his cheek twitched as something akin to concern showed on his face.

As he finished his food and wine and repacked the basket, she tried not to stare at him. She dreaded getting back into that carriage where her stomach churned much like the carriage wheels on the uneven roadway.

To her astonishment, when they reached the coach, his lordship changed seats. In a move completely uncharacteristic for a peer of the realm, he took the seat with his back to the front. *On the seat where she had sat since departing in London.* Her heartbeat began to roar. Was he trying to establish intimacy with her by sitting beside her? She had been so certain that he had no designs on her honor. What would she do were he to try to force himself on her? There was no chance her strength could overcome his. He was a tall man; she was small. Even if she were to scream, the coachman's allegiance was to the man who employed him. He was not likely to jeopardize his position for the sake of an insignificant woman.

She was terrified.

Chapter Five

Her heartbeat thundered.

He offered a smile. "I have it on good authority that sitting in a front-facing seat is better for one who complains of carriage sickness. Please, sit where I was sitting."

She had grossly misjudged him. In so many ways. Nothing she had been able to observe of him reinforced his reputation as a rake. He could not have behaved in a more gentlemanly manner. She wondered how many other earls would concern themselves over the discomfort of an insignificant spinster. How was it he could so accurately tap into the feelings of others? He'd even known she would be appreciative of fine Palladian architecture.

"That's very kind of you," she said, scooting onto the seat he'd formerly occupied. "It might seem like a small thing, but I assure you that facing forward makes a tremendous difference in the misery gauge."

"Forgive me for not thinking of it sooner," he said as the coachman cracked his whip, and the horses sputtered forward.

"But you had no idea I'm cursed with so sensitive a stomach until I told you at lunch."

He shrugged. "I tend to behave in too lordly a fashion."

"How long since you inherited?"

"I succeeded to the earldom nearly ten years ago, but I was an arrogant viscount before that."

She laughed good naturedly. He no longer seemed so arrogant. Were it not for his physical attributes, she could have thought of him as a benevolent uncle. His extremely satisfactory appearance, though, reminded her of just what a desirable man he was and what an undesirable woman she was. "I did think you arrogant, but not now."

"I am beastly arrogant, but today I'm on my best behavior. Can't have Devere or your brother challenging me to a duel."

She favored him with a smile. As much as she adored her cousin Devere, she seriously doubted he would endanger his life for his mousy cousin. She was fully aware that it was her lack of beauty—not the protection of her brother or cousin—that preserved her virtue from one of the most notorious rakes in London. Still, she had a difficult time equating this courtly gentleman sitting across from her with the scandalous man she'd read about in the newspapers.

She started to state that she wasn't worthy of anyone fighting a duel over, but she stopped herself. To deprecate herself, even if it were true, would only accentuate her deficiencies to this man, and it suddenly seemed important to her that she not be a source of further pity. More importantly, she wished he could see her in a favorable light, however impossible that might be.

All she had to recommend her was a fine wardrobe and the fact she came from one of England's oldest aristocratic families. She was also considered quite clever, but that was a detriment when trying to find a marriage partner. Men did not prize intelligent women.

So she said nothing.

He must have taken her silence for disinterest in conversation for he pulled back his curtain and gazed from the coach window. She did the same, and a long period of silence followed.

Just after dusk, they came to a coaching inn where two adjacent rooms had been procured by the earl's valet, who had arrived first, along with Hannah. Lucy's maid was already putting clean linens on her mistress's bed.

His lordship stopped in front of Lucy's chamber door and turned to her. "Dinner will be served in my parlor in an hour, Miss Beresford."

Without thinking what she was doing, she nodded. Now that she was on solid ground without the churning in her stomach, she allowed herself to contemplate food. She could not remember when she had ever been hungrier. She could eagerly devour whatever was served—even stewed eel, which she had always abhorred.

In her chamber, a corner room with two tall windows, Lucy spoke to Hannah. "I need you to assist me into something nice for dinner. I will join his lordship in the adjacent parlor."

Hannah spun around. "Why did you not tell me that lord you'd be traveling with was sinfully handsome?"

"What does that have to do with anything?"

"I would have spent more time on yer hair this morning. And I would have insisted you wear the blue dress."

"Surely you don't think a sinfully handsome earl would take the slightest notice of me!"

Hannah stood back and whisked her gaze over Lucy. Hannah had come to Lucy just before her presentation nearly seven years earlier. Though the ginger-haired maid was the same age as Lucy, she had two previous years of experience as a lady's maid before arriving at the Beresford household. She'd come highly recommended after her young mistress, the wife of a wealthy brewer, died in childbed. Though the deceased had not mingled with the *ton*, she was noted for her beauty and style.

"One can hope," Hannah said. "You've got no competition during this journey. It's time to rope his attentions. Yer no beauty, but you ain't ugly, either."

Lucy glared. "You forget, Hardnosed Hannah, I'm a betrothed woman."

"A betrothed woman who's going to give that no-good Mr. Hutchinson an ultimatey."

"Ultimatum."

"Well, you just sit down and let Hannah fashion yer hair. And yer going to wear that blue dress to dinner tonight and dazzle his handsome lordship."

If only...

Lucy felt terribly guilty for even thinking of Lord Montague in such terms. After all, she was betrothed to his dearest friend. And it wasn't as if the earl could ever be attracted to her, even in the impossible eventuality that she were the only woman in his sphere, say after an unimagined disaster like the Great Fire of London. And it wasn't just her lack of beauty that accounted for her lack of desirability. She was deficient in so many ways. Those from London must find this young woman from the country exceedingly boring, and her experience with men was nonexistent. Her only claim to skill lay in her knowledge of politics. Though it was inferior to that of men who served in Parliament, she knew it exceeded that of most women.

She plopped onto a chair and allowed Hannah to comb and curl and coax her hair into something remarkably pretty.

"Speaking of handsome, the earl's valet, Mr. Cummings, could put his shoes under my bed anytime."

"Hannah!"

The maid tossed her head back in laughter. "You must see for yerself how handsome Mr. Cummings is. I felt like a fine lady, riding with him all day. He has a way about him that makes me feel . . ." She pursed her lips. "Pretty, actually."

"You are pretty."

"Aw, yer just being nice."

"I am not. Have you and I ever flattered each other?"

Hannah shrugged. "When I first came to you, I attempted flattery, trying to get in yer good graces, but I soon abandoned it."

Lucy smiled.

"Now let's get you into that blue dress. Nothing's more flattering on you than that."

After Hannah had assisted her into the pale blue gown, she stood back to gaze at her mistress. "I'll tell you one thing. There ain't no beauty who's got eyes as pretty as yours."

Lucy could not deny that not only were her eyes her best feature—they truly were uncommonly lovely. They were large and fringed with lashes a bit longer than other women's, and she'd been told their color was everything from robin's egg to sapphire, though she failed to see any resemblance between the two.

"Now you go next door and make a fine impression on that earl," Hannah instructed.

"Is it not I who should be giving the orders?"

"Yer too shy by half." Hannah then peered at herself in the looking glass.

That must mean Hannah was going to be eating with his lordship's valet. "Will you be dining with Mr. Cummings?"

A sly smile on her lightly freckled face, Hannah gave a sheepish nod. "I've got to remember to keep my mouth closed when I chew my food. Mr. Cummings does act like a fine gentleman."

"I'm certain you'll comport yourself well."

Hannah's brows lowered. "What's comfort got to do with it?"

"*Comport*. That means, well, it means you will behave in an agreeable fashion."

Hannah moved toward the door. "I'll do my best."

Lucy drew a breath. She really was starving, and she wanted to spend more time with his lordship, but dare she eat? What if she spilled the contents of her stomach in his fine coach tomorrow? Perhaps just a wee bite.

As dull as Miss Beresford was, Monty preferred her companionship over eating alone. Being one of eight children, he was used to being surrounded by people. He could not abide a quiet house.

Exactly an hour after they parted outside her chamber, a timid knock sounded at his door. When he opened it, he was almost taken aback. Miss Beresford looked . . . not exactly pretty but something akin to it. In a vague way. Certainly she looked lovelier than she had during the many hours spent in his coach. What was different?

Her hair was perfection, as was her blue dress. She still was uncommonly pale and slender, but now it brought to mind the delicacy of Dresden porcelain—something too fragile to touch. And he could not help but notice how the blue in the dress complemented her eyes. Extraordinary eyes. "Do come in, Miss Beresford."

Like her selection of clothing, there was grace and elegance in her movement as she came to sit at the Pembroke table where he pulled out a chair for her. She glanced nervously about the candlelit chamber before speaking in a quivering voice. "I should die of mortification if anyone were to ever learn that I was alone here with you."

"I do hope you know that no one will ever learn of it from me."

She finally met his gaze. "I do. After all, you gave me your word, and I believe you. You've given me no reason to doubt your sincerity."

It was a major victory that she'd answered him in complete sentences. Perhaps she was growing more comfortable in his presence. He was also relieved that she trusted him. With all those loosely veiled references to his paramours in the London newspapers, he could understand why a maiden would fear for her virtue in his presence.

Mindful of her affliction, he had ordered simple fare. No rich sauces tonight. A simple English meat pie centered the small table, where two places had been set. He poured wine into a glass and handed it to her.

"Allow me to say you look lovely tonight, Miss Beresford." Oddly, he meant those words.

Her lashes lowered. "You're very kind, my lord."

He smiled and held up his glass. "May I offer a toast? Here's to the success of our mission to find your missing Mr. Thomas Hutchinson."

Their glasses clicked together, and a smile played at her soft pink lips.

"I'm expecting you to eat tonight," he said in an authoritative tone.

That look of fear returned to her face. "I will try a few bites, but that's all."

"I am relieved to hear that. I shouldn't want Devere's cousin to waste away whilst in my care."

She cut the pie into four sections, then cut one of those sections in half and scooped it onto her plate. He helped himself to two sections.

"Confess, Miss Beresford, you have to be famished."

She giggled. Even though he knew her to be in her middle twenties, she was possessed of a girlish voice. "I cannot deny it. I had meant to wait until we reached Bath before eating, but the very idea of food weakened all my resolve. I will own, I've never been so hungry."

She placed a dainty bite into her mouth. Where her bite was no larger than that offered an infant, the huge scoop he was shoveling into his mouth made him feel like a glutton. In truth, in contrast to her, he felt gargantuan.

When they finished eating, he asked her to join him in front of the fire. The night had grown cold, and sitting near the hearth and finishing their decanter of port held allure. A pity the lady wasn't more interesting.

He was careful not to sit next to her on the parlor's sofa. It would come off as too intimate. Instead, he pulled over one of the wooden chairs from the table and faced her. To his astonishment, she initiated conversation. "I've read about your work in the House of Lords."

A woman was interested in matters political? That was a rarity. He had yet to meet the woman who could converse intelligently about such matters. He raised a brow. "Then I take it you have also followed the progress of Mr. Hutchinson."

"Indeed I have, and it's occurred to me that the two of you support the same progressive reforms."

This was the second time in less than a minute the lady had astonished him. "You really do follow parliamentary occurrences."

"It's a subject that interests me. Because of that, I will own that I already knew a great deal about Lady Harriet's bridegroom. From what I've read of him, he's highly respected. Still, I wanted to meet him for myself. I wished to see that he properly values my cousin."

"You should have no uneasiness on that account. He's a fine man. If he pledged to love your cousin, he would not hesitate to lay down his life for her. And in politics, he will go far. Tell me, did you become interested in government because of Devere?"

"Partly. I'm very proud of my cousin and what he's been able to accomplish since he entered public service."

"As you should be." The Beresford family had been pillars of Whig society for the past century. As had his family.

"I confess I was relieved to learn that you and Reluctant Bridegroom augmented your... ahem, *pleasure pursuits* with more important matters."

Pleasure pursuits was a tactful way of acknowledging the men's many dalliances with women of questionable repute. A pity she knew about those.

His somber gaze met hers. "One mustn't believe everything one reads in the newspapers." He may not have hesitated to enjoy himself, but if he had alliances with half the women who'd been linked with him in the periodicals, he would never have had time to take his seat in the House of Lords.

"That's good to know. I'm also happy to know that you and Mr. Hutchinson are intent on limiting the funds given the Regent via the Civil List."

She really was remarkably well acquainted with his work in Parliament. "Our refusal to bow to the Royal whim is what makes us stand apart from the Tories."

"I would say that's not all, but it's admirable."

Perhaps Miss Beresford was not as dull as he'd thought. For the next hour, neither of them wanted for conversation. They spoke of penal reform and rotten boroughs and universal education, and not for a moment did they flounder for something to discuss. There was little difference between conversing with Miss Beresford here in a country inn in England's heartland than in speaking with fellow parliamentarians at a gathering at Brook's.

⋙✦⋘

THEIR CONVERSATION NEVER stopped throughout the following day though he could tell her stomach was queasy. That afternoon, she begged for the carriage to stop. She had eaten neither breakfast nor lunch, but still he could tell she was unwell.

She'd managed to walk some distance away from the coach when she bent over and retched. He felt beastly.

When she rejoined him, she was, if possible, even paler than normal. Something within him melted. He fought the fleeting desire to draw her into his arms and offer comfort.

"Is it all right if I have the coachman proceed, or should you like to sit here while your stomach settles?" he asked, his voice sympathetic.

"I'm all right now."

She may no longer be nauseated, but he could tell she was weak. Very weak. "Are you sure?"

She nodded.

He tapped the roof to signal the coachman to move.

"I'm sorry for being such a ninny," she said.

"You have nothing for which you need to apologize. It's I who feel like an ogre for allowing you to become so miserable."

"You had nothing to do with my misery." A moment later, she added, "In fact, I can't remember when I've ever enjoyed myself so thoroughly. Except for the digestive difficulties."

He almost laughed at her remark, but there was nothing laughable about her sickness. "Pray, what could possibly make this trip in any way delightful?"

She thought a moment before she responded. "I suppose it's that I've never before been on my own with no parent or guardian to tell me what to do, how to act, what I could not do. Also, I've never been able to converse alone with a man before, and I find it much more interesting than speaking of frocks and poetry."

When put like that, he supposed this trip had been enjoyable for her. Her candidness with him made him feel as if he'd fed the masses with a single fish. She'd gone from one-syllable answers to revealing some of her innermost thoughts—at least thoughts of political reform—with him.

He was almost disappointed when his coach pulled up in front of his family home on the Royal Crescent.

Chapter Six

The Royal Crescent, Lucy knew, was the most select residential terrace in all of Bath, but the houses there were no nicer than the fine London townhouses owned by the various branches of the Beresford family. What made the Royal Crescent so sought after was its prospect proudly looking down its (mostly) aristocratic nose over the vast green blanket of Crescent Fields from end to end of that regal curved street.

When her papa had come to Bath for the waters the year before he died, the Duke of York himself was taking up residence right next door to Lord Montague's house near the crescent's center.

In addition to having its royal associations to recommend it, Lucy had been told the crescent was situated within relatively short walking distance of all the watering city's attractions: the Pump Room, the cathedral, Theatre Royal, and the Upper Assembly Rooms.

As Lord Montague showed Lucy around his well-appointed house, she found it to be in elegant taste and free of one's everyday clutter. It brought to mind a miniature Versailles—another place she'd only visited in books. But tasteful French influences in gilded mirrors and furnishings, rich jewel-toned silks, and delicate porcelain in bold colors like turquoise, apple green, and fuchsia could be found in every chamber.

His lordship showed her to the chamber that had belonged to his mother. "I would suggest you sleep here," he said.

Nothing could be lovelier than the pale-yellow chamber with its high poster bed draped with more pale-yellow silks and soft greenery in the papered walls. Lord Montague had been careful to stand in the doorway, not to come into the intimacy of the bedchamber with the blushing maiden.

Before she could become too embarrassed, he said, "I know you must be starving. Let us go to the dinner room now."

That chamber with its crimson damask walls and glittering candelabra dazzled. A variety of dishes awaited discovery beneath silver salvers, but the smell of French sauces already delighted.

He scooted out a chair for her to the right of his seat at the head of the table. He'd sent ahead his staff by post chaise, so that they could have a meal ready to serve.

Now she could indulge herself! She matched Lord Montague bite for bite.

"You really do eat!" he said.

"I told you."

He gave her a searing look, one that made her feel again as if she were being undressed by his brooding eyes. "Yes. You said you were trying to gain *curvature*." His glance moved to her partially exposed breasts that tucked into her gown's narrow bodice.

The very mention of her curvature, however modest it was, sent the heat rising to her cheeks. "You don't have to recall my exact words."

"Forgive me." There was not a speck of remorse in his voice.

Unlike the previous night, as soon as he ate, he got up and took his leave—much to her disappointment.

※

Monty did not want Miss Beresford to know he intended to call on

Mrs. Colecott that very evening. If he had his way, Lucy Beresford would never know about Hutch's association with the promiscuous actress.

A few inquiries resulted in Monty learning that Mrs. Colecott was at lodgings on Queen Square. A nice address. Hutch must have been most generous with his newest inamorata.

When Monty called at her house, he was shown into the drawing room while the actress was notified of his arrival. Gratified that she was home, he sat on a shabby chair with faded upholstery and waited for a considerable time before the lady appeared.

He had never seen Henrietta Colecott up close, only from his box a few hundred feet above the stage at Drury Lane. When she finally entered the chamber, he noted that she possessed the body of a Venus with bountiful curvature, but even in the evening's candlelight, up close her face looked old. Harsh. Her fleshy chin made her look twice the age of Hutch's fiancée.

He stood when she entered the chamber, and though he greeted her amiably, he was thinking how unfavorably she compared to Miss Beresford. One was hardened by age, the other flush with innocence and virtue. How could Hutch prefer the former?

"Please, Lord Montague, won't you sit?" The actress waved a bejeweled hand at the well-worn sofa. "I beg that you overlook the condition of the furnishings. One has little control when one is letting a house for so short a period."

"Most importantly, you've come to a good address that's convenient to everything that matters."

After she sat across from him, he got to the purpose of his visit. "I was told that my friend Thomas Hutchinson asked you to meet him here in Bath."

"He did, though not directly. He wrote me a letter. Which I admit I thought strange. In the five months we've been ... together, he never once sent me a letter. We had our set days, days when we could be together, days when I wasn't performing."

Nights more likely. "And he's here with you now?"

Her face saddened. She looked softer then, like a concerned mother. "He's never shown."

Her candidness demonstrated the level of her concern over his friend. Monty's chest clenched. "And you've not heard from him any further?"

She shook her head somberly.

Something's terribly wrong.

"I've thought and thought about it," she said. "When I received the note, it had been several days since I'd seen him. He'd uncharacteristically missed coming to me on Tuesday night. I heard nothing. Then out of the blue, I received the letter. I cannot even vouch that it was in his hand. Now I'm wondering if some wicked hoax has been played upon me."

Monty was beginning to feel like Miss Beresford had felt in the moving coach. Sickness stirred in his stomach. Something must have happened to Hutchinson. "Do you still have the letter?" Monty would recognize the hand of his best friend as surely as he did that of his own sisters and brothers.

"I do. Would you care to see it?"

"Indeed I would."

She rang for a servant. "Please tell my maid to bring my letter box to me straight away."

A moment later, Mrs. Colecott retrieved the letter from a mother-of-pearl box which she opened with a key kept on her person. He could well imagine a woman of her vast experience would preserve a store of intimate letters from various lovers throughout the years and wish to keep them safe.

She handed the single page to him. As soon as he read it, he realized it had not been penned by his friend. Though the person who wrote it was familiar enough with Hutchinson's hand to forge an adequate facsimile, it could not have been written by this woman's current protector. This letter writer had spelled Wednesday correctly, but Hutch had never done so. He'd always written it *Windsday.*

"Well?" she asked.

He glanced up at her solemn face. "It's not from Hutchinson."

Her green eyes began to glisten. "Someone has played a cruel hoax upon me."

"I don't think that was the intent."

"Then what do you think?"

"There are details surrounding the circumstances of his sudden absence that are troubling. I think someone is attempting to cover up our friend's disappearance."

She grabbed at her chest, wincing. "Something's happened to my dear Tommy!"

That was Monty's greatest fear. Someone had taken pains to make it appear Hutch had not disappeared. Why?

No good would be served by further worrying the distraught actress. He stood. "Be assured I will find out, and when I do, I shall let you know."

Then he took his leave.

―――※―――

EVEN THOUGH MONTY knew in his gut that Hutch was not in Bath, he could not capitulate in his fervent search. So he went first to Mrs. Starr's gambling establishment. His inquiries there resulted only in the knowledge that his friend had not been there.

Next, Monty strolled up Great Pulteney Street to the Sydney Hotel, the only place Hutchinson stayed when the Montague residence in the Royal Crescent was not available. Though it was late, an attendant there confirmed that not only was Mr. Hutchinson not in residence, but he had not stayed there at any time in the past several weeks.

While Monty was at the hotel, he paid for his own night's lodgings then continued his search.

Each negative inquiry intensified the dread that strummed through Monty. Desperate now, his last resort was the city's brothel. Monty himself had never been there, but he knew it was located just off Laura Place. He crossed the river via the Pulteney Bridge. All the shops along the Adam-built bridge were now closed. Soon he arrived at the establishment known as Mrs. Henry's. Of course, there was no sign in front of the modest-looking house that indicated the nature of the establishment, but the pair of lanterns flanking the door were painted bright red.

He climbed the steps and knocked, and then presented his card to the very large footman who answered. This was one of those circumstances when being a Lord Something or Other always got underlings' attention. Were he actually a patron here, he would not have identified himself, but tonight he needed to loosen tongues. "It's worth a crown to me to find out if my friend has been here recently."

The footman's brows lifted, and a smile tweaked at his lips. "Your friend's name, my lord?"

"Mr. Thomas Hutchinson."

The footman pursed his lips in exaggerated thought. "I've not 'eard of the gent. He's Quality like yerself?"

Monty nodded. "He's my age and almost as tall as me. His hair is the same brown as yours."

"That don't sound familiar to me, but allow me to make inquiries."

He directed Monty to a small, sparsely furnished morning room off the narrow entry corridor, and Monty waited in an armchair there. It must be a slow night. No sound, other than the footman's tread on the stairway, could be heard. No tinkling of brandy glasses. No feminine giggles or deep male voices. No thumping coming from the floor above.

Ten minutes later, the footman reappeared, shaking his head. "I've asked each lady here, including Mrs. 'Enry, but it doesn't seem yer Mr. Hutchinson's been here."

Monty's inscrutable face did not reveal his inner turmoil as he stood and offered the footman a crown. "I thank you for your efforts."

On the way to the Sydney Hotel, Monty thought about what he would tell Miss Beresford. Certainly he would not mention either Mrs. Colecott or Mrs. Henry's. Was there anything he could say or do that would protect her from the mounting worry that consumed him?

Were it not for the forged letter—which he was powerless to explain—suicide would be looking more and more likely. No one Monty had spoken to in London knew Hutch's whereabouts, and this trip to Bath had turned up nothing. Which left his country home, Siddons. He prayed Hutch had gone home to escape his gambling debts. It was Monty's last hope of finding his friend alive. Monty must go there and find out, one way or another.

And he was determined that Miss Beresford would stay in Bath.

⁂

THANKFUL THAT LORD Montague's servants had lighted a fire in the chamber she would sleep in, Lucy had intended to sit before the hearth and attempt to record the day's events and her impressions of it in her journal, but doing so proved impossible. Her thoughts kept reverting to her missing fiancé. And to his closest friend. She felt shamefully guilty for not being more concerned over Mr. Hutchinson's absence—and for being so frightfully attracted to Lord Montague.

How could it be that three days earlier she had been terrified over the prospect of meeting the notorious Lord Montague, the greatest rake in all of London, and now she craved every moment spent in his company?

Was inherent charm what made rakes so attractive to women?

Although, she had to admit she had seen nothing about his lordship which pointed to him even being a rake. Quite the opposite. The man was a paragon of gentility. Could it be that newspaper accounts were not always accurate? Lord Montague could not have treated her with greater respect had she been his favorite sister. In fact, his entire demeanor toward her was what one would expect from a close family member. Her own dear, elder brother was just as solicitous of her welfare as Lord Montague had been.

Though she was comforted by Lord Montague's kindly treatment, Lucy abhorred the notion he could think of her as a sister. She wished she could be an object of desire to him, even though she knew such a wild wish could never come to fruition. And the very thought of such a betrayal of Mr. Hutchinson shamed her.

She abandoned her pen, climbed upon the late Lady Montague's bed, and lay there in the darkness as she listened to the crackling fire, hour after hour, until the crackle dissipated into smoldering embers. Each thought, whether a fragment or a fully fleshed out remembrance or idea, centered on the provocative Lord Montague.

She was still awake when Hannah entered her chamber early the following morning. "I see you've been at the diarrhea again."

Lucy's mouth gaped open in shock. Then she noticed her maid's gaze had flitted to the unfinished journal entry. She frowned. "Diary. Not diarrhea."

"You knew what I was talking about, did you not?" The maid squinted at her.

With an exasperated harrumph, Lucy sprang from the bed to begin her morning toilette. After helping Lucy dress in a muslin dress sprigged with tiny blue flowers, Hannah sculpted her mistress's hair into something fashionable and flattering.

"Is Lord Montague to be here this morning?" the maid asked.

"I'm not sure. He left in rather a hurry last night, as if he had to attend to pressing business."

"Course he did. He had to find his friend, the man yer betrothed to."

Lucy was not about to confess to Hannah her deep disappointment that his lordship had not lingered with her after dinner. Hannah must be right. He was merely anxious to find Mr. Hutchinson. For that, she ought to be grateful.

A knock sounded at her chamber door. "Lord Montague wishes to see your mistress," the butler said when Hannah responded. Her heartbeat accelerating, Lucy nodded and left the bedchamber.

Lord Montague stood at the base of the stairway, hat in hand, as he looked up at her. Her pulse quickened—not from the excitement of seeing the handsome earl but from disappointment. He hadn't given the butler his hat, so he must not be meaning to stay.

"Good day to you, my lord," she greeted warily.

"And to you, Miss Beresford."

"I have not broken the fast yet. Won't you join me in your breakfast room for a bite?"

"I cannot stay. I came only to tell you that I must leave Bath at once."

She felt as if she'd been slapped. Did this man intend to leave her stranded here in Bath, alone and without one familiar face? She was terrified.

As difficult as it was for Lucy to be assertive, she forced herself to be so. "I must insist you take me with you."

Chapter Seven

"It pains me to leave you here, but it's for your own good. I'm obliged to leave Bath at once." Lord Montague paused. "Because of the large quantities of food you consumed last night, I am concerned."

"You fear I'll soil your fine coach?"

"I don't give a fig about the coach. It's you I care about."

Her heartbeat exploded. She knew he didn't really mean he cared about her in the way a man cares about a woman he loves. He meant he worried about her affliction. Still, just hearing those words on his lips touched her profoundly. Other than her dear papa, no man had ever told her he cared about her. Her gaze lifted to his. "I appreciate your concern, my lord, and I cannot dispute the merit of your fears. Nevertheless, I cannot continue on in Bath alone."

"It won't be for long. I go to Siddons, then I'll return for you. That will give you time to . . . schedule a fast."

Her determination to be forceful faded under the wisdom of his suggestion, but wise or not, she knew she must refuse to continue on in Bath. More than her abhorrence to staying alone here, she felt compelled to aid Lord Montague in locating her missing fiancé. No longer could she be content to wait on Mr. Hutchinson. Her very future depended on her ability to confront Reluctant Bridegroom. Soon. Whenever he was found she must be on the spot.

She squared her shoulders, lifted her chin, met his somber gaze, and spoke with defiance. "Fast or no fast, I will be ready in ten minutes."

His dark eyes flashed with anger, and he spoke stiffly. "Very well, Miss Beresford. I'll alert my servants."

<hr />

WHAT A TRANSFORMATION had come over Miss Beresford! What had happened to that docile woman who had asked him to call upon her in London just a few days previously, barely able to nervously utter more than a single word? Never would he have thought that shy, skinny spinster capable of barking out orders to him. And never would he have believed himself capable of acquiescing to her demands. Yet here he was, once again allowing her to sit in his coach's front-facing seat as they sped to Siddons.

Unlike the last day they had spent madly conversing on all things political, today the coach's silence was like a mournful vigil. Monty was determined not to initiate conversation. Instead, he demonstrated a great deal of interest in observing the passing countryside and would occasionally steal a glance at her to gauge her physical tolerance for the bumpy road. The farther they went, the whiter her already-pale complexion became.

It would serve her right if she spilled the contents of her stomach. She should have heeded his advice to stay in Bath. She'd eaten enough the previous evening to have fed two hungry farm workers. He'd truly had her best interest in mind when he'd asked her to remain in Bath today.

Maddening woman! Her misery must be growing for she closed her eyes, and her face grew ashen.

In spite of his resolve to remain impervious to her misery, he did become concerned. Before the sun was lodged in the sky overhead, she clutched at her stomach. "Please, stop the coach!"

After instructing the coachman, Monty was not about to wait for the man to dismount from the box and come to open the door. Instead, he leapt from his seat, threw open the coach door, and stood on the solid dirt to lift her down. She thereupon raced away to retch.

He felt beastly. He had never been able to ignore the suffering of any creature.

When she returned to the coach, her face blanched, she regarded him through narrowed eyes. "Don't. Say. Anything."

Their gazes met and held. "You misjudge me if you think I could gloat over your infirmity."

A sliver of a smile crept across her wan face. "Forgive me."

"I truly am sorry about your affliction."

"As am I," she said with resignation.

Once he was assured that she was feeling better, he decided he owed her an explanation on why he had to leave Bath so suddenly. Still, it would not be a complete explanation since he couldn't tell her about Mrs. Colecott. And he hated like the devil to be the source of her mounting fears that her fiancé may, indeed, have killed himself.

"I made inquiries last night about Hutchinson. I went to all the places I knew he frequented and a few I only suspected he might, and no one has seen him."

"We feared as much."

He drew a deep breath and continued. "I cannot conceal from you my worry."

Her brows lowered. "You think something's happened to him?" She went still and finally lifted her anxious gaze to his. "You think he may have killed himself after his extensive losses?"

"That's what I fear, and I won't rest easy until I investigate every source."

"That's why we're going to Mr. Hutchinson's family home? Your last hope is that we will find him at Siddons?" She sounded hopeful.

He wished he possessed this woman's optimism. "Yes."

***

IT WAS DUSK when they came to the Somerset village of Siddons. The village owed its name to the nearby Elizabethan house that had been home to the Hutchinson family for more than two hundred years.

Her family had spent a delightful Christmas at Siddons with the Hutchinson family five years previously. It had been such a happy time before each of the betrothed had lost their parents. Something in her heart caught at the morose memory of loved ones since gone. *Please, God, don't let Mr. Hutchinson meet the same fate as our parents.* He was too young, too handsome, too vital to die.

She had known that long-ago Christmas that one day she would be mistress of Siddons, but she had thought it would be many years hence before that sad succession would occur.

As the turrets and ogees of Siddons came into view, she no longer experienced a thrill at the thought of becoming its mistress. Too many conflicting emotions had stolen away the sweet anticipation associated with marriage to her missing fiancé. Days ago, she'd had doubts about the union, owing to his continued neglect of her, his failure to mature, and his mounting gaming losses. Those concerns had now been superseded by fears of his death. Now she could forget the deficiencies of Mr. Hutchinson, if only he were safe and well. Now, she would eagerly wed him.

Still, she was just as impressed with Siddons on this warm spring day as she'd been when it was dusted with snow and surrounded by winter's barren trees. Siddons was one of the loveliest ancestral homes in all of Somerset. If she remembered correctly, it featured over 125 chambers. The discomfort of the austere, near-freezing rooms of December was more than offset by the beauty of the Capability Brown landscape of rolling hills, well-placed lakes with hump-back stone bridges and low-hanging willow branches skimming the water's surface.

In fact, Lucy decided as they drove toward the house, it was far lovelier now than it had been that winter when she had first visited. Every imaginable shade of green was reflected in the plentiful trees whose sizes and shapes varied as much as the colors. Were her mission of a different nature, she would have enjoyed stopping here for several days to explore the beautiful countryside surrounding Siddons.

If Mr. Hutchinson was here, perhaps they could celebrate with a satisfying stay at Siddons. As they neared the home's circular entrance drive, though, her stomach stirred. Her heartbeat drummed madly. She was shaken by a horrifying conviction that they would not find Mr. Hutchinson here.

The footman showed no signs that he recognized either Lucy or her name. However, he readily recognized his master's closest friend. His face brightened when he saw the earl. "Lord Montague! What a pleasure to see you. Mr. Hutchinson will be sorry to have missed you."

Her stomach dropped. She and Lord Montague exchanged somber expressions. "Mr. Hutchinson's not here?" his lordship asked, disappointment in his voice.

"No, my lord. I thought he needed to be in London to attend the House of Commons."

"That's correct," the earl said. "But we've been in Bath and wanted to stop by here in the hopes of seeing Mr. Hutchinson," he hedged. "When was he last here?"

The footman, who looked to be the same age as Lord Montague, puckered his lips in thought. "Don't know precisely. About two or three months ago."

She could tell by the solemnity of his expression, her traveling companion was vastly disappointed. He thanked the footman and turned back toward his carriage.

Her queasiness from the coach ride was magnified tenfold now because of her fears for her fiancé's well-being. "I know you don't wish to utter it, but it's looking more and more as if Mr. Hutchinson may have taken his own life."

"You're right. I cannot give voice to such speculation." His demeanor, his stiffness, and especially his quivering voice bespoke his chilling fears.

He told the coachman to take them back to the posting inn they had observed in the village of Siddons. Between Siddons Hall and the inn, not a single word was spoken.

But it apparently was not an idle silence. His mind must have gone off on still another hopeful explanation for his friend's absence, for he presented his shocking theory to her when she came to his private parlor at the Siddons coaching inn for dinner.

Chapter Eight

At the White Knight posting inn, Monty once again invited Miss Beresford to his chamber for dinner. The lady came but refused to eat. "I'll eat in London tomorrow night. I am assured I will not expire from two days of fasting." She eyed the decanter. "If you permit, I will have a glass of wine."

He poured it into her glass. "I feel beastly eating in front of you."

"Please don't. My digestive difficulties have stolen away my appetite today. It would be impossible for me to even be tempted by your food."

He eyed her like a stern father. "Forgive me if I don't believe you. Your stomach has to be raw from emptiness."

"Oh, it is gnawing, but the jostling outweighs the gnawing!"

"Before I eat, I want to share something with you."

"You've thought of something else to explore?"

"Perhaps." He frowned. "First, I want to tell you that when I decided to go to Siddons it was to ascertain if my friend might have committed suicide."

"I know."

"The pity of it is that I still cannot rule it out." It grieved him to bring up so horrifying a prospect to the man's fiancé, but Monty was no longer so convinced that his friend had killed himself.

"If one were intent on committing suicide, what method would be preferrable?" she asked.

He shrugged. "I would want something quick. Like leaping from the top of St. Paul's."

"But we would have known it if he'd done that."

"Yes."

"What manner of death by one's own hand might delay discovery of the body?" she asked.

"Perhaps jumping off one of the Thames' bridges in the dark of night. Hutch, you know, was unable to swim."

She nodded. "That's the same thing I was thinking. Would it not be possible, then, for the body not to be discovered for up to two weeks?"

"I'm no expert, but I'd say, depending on the congestion on the riverway, that's possible."

"A determined person could even tie something like a brick to one's foot to ensure he didn't pop up."

He drew a deep breath as his lashes lowered. He was incapable of acknowledging her comment. It was a moment before he finally met her solemn gaze.

"I know this is as disagreeable a subject for you as it is for me," she said. "But I know one of Devere's grooms has a brother with some sort of occupation helping on a boat that scavenges the Thames from London to Windsor. Perhaps we can learn from him if he knows of any bodies having washed up in the past week or so."

His stomach flipped at the very notion that his vibrant friend could have been reduced to a bloated corpse. "It's an avenue we must explore," he said in a morose voice.

"Forgive me for this morbid conversation," she said. "Please feel free to go on with another, more hopeful theory about Mr. Hutchinson's disappearance if you have one."

It only just occurred to him that Hutch's disappearance might have something to do with his duties at the Foreign Office. Why had Monty not considered that earlier? He might have saved himself this fruitless trip to Bath as well as to Siddons. "Whether my newest theory has merit or not remains to be seen."

"What, pray tell, have you remembered?" she asked.

"It may be nothing, but Hutch holds a position at the Foreign Office. I assumed he pushed paper around on the days he served—indeed he always said as much himself . . ."

"But now?"

"It's just possible he might have been involved in clandestine activities with our enemies."

"You mean like a spy?"

He shrugged. "I have no evidence of it. It's just a theory—a theory I mean to explore." A theory he hoped to God had more merit than his persistent, numbing fear that Hutch might have taken his own life.

"Did you not say you and Mr. Hutchinson have shared everything since you were lads?"

"We have. That's one of the difficulties I'm having with the suicide theory. I think he'd at least have left me a personal note if he were going to take his life. I will own, the single sentence I read in his library could have been intended as such, but it was strange. I really don't know how to interpret it. I do believe he'd have written to me to explain if he meant to do himself harm." His voice cracked. "Suicide."

"If I were going to kill myself, I would most definitely have written more than one sentence—and not a cryptic one, at that—to explain my actions."

"Precisely." His voice brightened. "Now that I'm thinking on it, though, I realize there were times he was particularly evasive about his duties for the Foreign Office. I never pressed him on it, however—I simply assumed. But I do know that patriots engaged in such activities."

"Like spying?"

"Yes. Spies for the Crown are sworn to secrecy. Hutch may have his faults, but if he took an oath, I know he would honor it. Even if it meant withholding the truth from me."

She frowned. "Your opinion of his honor may be colored by affection. I'm beginning to think Reluctant Bridegroom had no intentions of ever honoring his vow to my father."

"The promise to marry you?"

She nodded somberly. "I will not put you in the uncomfortable position of having to answer questions about what Mr. Hutchinson might have shared with you about our betrothal."

Sadly for Miss Beresford, Hutch never spoke of his betrothal but went about his merry way as if it had never occurred. But Monty would choose to be hanged with the criminals at Tyburn rather than admit that to the unfortunate lady.

She must have sensed his discomfort over the subject for she returned to his theory about Hutchinson's covert duties. "I am wondering how Mr. Hutchinson's duties in the Foreign Office could have jeopardized him. After all, to my knowledge, he's never left the safety of London."

"I keep thinking about something Lord Stewart said at White's while in his cups a few weeks ago."

"Lord Stewart, the Foreign Secretary?" she asked.

He nodded. "He said there was evidence a high-ranking Napoleon sympathizer was ingratiating himself in our highest circles in order to carry out an assassination."

"Who's to be the victim?"

He shrugged. "He either doesn't know or wouldn't say."

"What would be the purpose of an assassination? We're currently at peace."

"Not as long as Napoleon draws breath. Apparently, there's a plan to liberate the former French emperor and then raise an army to defeat the British."

Her face collapsed. "After all those years of war and all those lives lost, how could anyone want to break the peace?"

"It's diabolical."

"Napoleon is diabolical!"

"Another subject on which you and I agree, Miss Beresford."

She settled back into her seat, deep in concentration for a few moments. "I wonder if Mr. Hutchinson discovered the identity of the . . . shall we call him the Evildoer?"

He chuckled. "We could."

"Would you not agree that would put Mr. Hutchinson's life in great jeopardy?"

"I would." How was it their roles had become reversed? He was answering in two syllables while she rattled on with the confidence of a lecturer at the Royal Society?

"It's a terrifying prospect." Her face fell.

The very thought of Hutchinson being dead sent Monty into blue devils. "If this theory should have any merit, I doubt there's anything we can do to save him."

"Because he'd already be dead," she murmured mournfully.

Her words were like the twist of a sword in his gut. "I shall proceed on the hope he's merely being held until the wicked deed is done."

"Then you and I will find him."

You and I? The woman's boldness had made her delusional. "This is not a task for a woman."

"You forget I have a deeply vested interest in Mr. Hutchinson."

There she was, once more being authoritarian toward him. He was an earl, for God's sake! How had she been able to so totally fool him into thinking her timid?

The pity of it was he could not deny the truth in her claim. Nevertheless, he was not about to permit her to traipse about London with him as he sought his missing friend.

"Hopefully," he said, looking to avoid another argument, "Hutch will be in London when we return."

If only he felt as hopeful as his own words.

※

LUCY WATCHED AS Cummings went into his lordship's adjoining bedchamber and closed the door behind him. "I do see what my maid meant when she spoke of your valet's attractiveness. It's easy to understand why she's smitten with him."

He popped a forkful of mutton into his mouth. "Is that so? I believe he remarked on your maid's attractiveness, also." His prurient mind fancied the servants' coach pounding along tomorrow beneath the weight of their lovemaking.

"Oh, Hardheaded Hannah is quite lovely."

An amused grin on his face, he stopped eating and regarded Miss Beresford. "Do you give your own colorful names to everyone?"

She shook her head. "Not everyone."

"I shall be offended if you have no name for me."

"Then you will have to be offended, my lord."

"Allow me to assist. Perhaps you could call me Lord Arrogant Earl. Or Scandalous Rake."

"Or if I were one of the ladies who capitulate to your flirtations, I could call you Magnificent Monty."

He nearly spit out his wine laughing. He was flattered that the adjective *magnificent* would even come to her mind in connection with him. Still, he knew she was not in the least drawn to him. He knew what attraction looked like and was accustomed to women fawning over him. Most women's lust for him—or his rank—was greater than their pride. Clearly, Miss Beresford was immune to whatever charms he possessed. "Hardly."

"I noticed the newspapers refer to you as *Monty*. Is that, indeed, what your friends call you?"

"It is. I inherited rather young, so I've held the Montague title for many years now. Monty is what your so-called Reluctant Bridegroom calls me."

Her tongue had gone silent. Was she embarrassed because she referred to him as *magnificent*? He must put her at ease. "Let me see . . . how can I refer to my traveling companion?" He thought for a moment. "Chameleon."

"Why would you call me that?"

"You go from docile to domineering in the blink of an eye."

Lashes lowered, color rose in her cheeks. She had pivoted back to bashful.

He hated being the source of her discomfort. "Forgive me if I've offended you."

It was a moment before she replied. "You do offend me, but I can't deny I have earned your moniker. You've found me out."

"Pray, don't tell me I'm the first to hit upon your little deception."

"It's no deception. A chameleon is exactly what I am. You see, I *am* painfully shy among strangers—and especially men. But once I'm comfortable with one, I can sometimes be overbearing."

"Then you must be possessed of supreme confidence."

She shrugged. "Confidence is usually the domain of those born to beauty and breeding. I have only the breeding, but I daresay my confidence comes from being the first—and cherished—daughter in a loving family."

"If my memory serves me correctly, your father was exceedingly devoted to you."

A solemn look on her delicate face, she nodded. "I've been blessed."

All of this morning's anger toward her evaporated under his present admiration. He admired truth, and this woman was probably the most honest woman he'd ever known. He changed the subject to politics, and they talked until his fire began to dim, sending her to her chamber.

But their conversation picked up again in the morning and all through the day until they arrived in London. They went straight to Hutch's house, hoping against hope that he had returned.

Chapter Nine

"You stay in the coach for now," Lord Montague told Lucy. "It will do your reputation no good to be seen exiting my coach with me, especially given that I am *not* the man to whom you're betrothed."

She nodded. Once he left the coach, she peered through the cracked opening of the velvet curtains. Sighing, she eyed Hutchinson House as would its future owner but with a tinge of doubt. Would she ever live here? It was well past time for Miss Lucy Beresford to marry and become mistress of her own home.

The brick house looked just as it had days earlier when she'd seriously perused it for the first time. Had that been just days ago? So much had occurred since then. She had become a different person over the course of the past week. On that day, she thought she knew about the man she had consented to marry. After all, they'd been betrothed for six years. In addition, she had read and committed to memory every article or gossip piece ever printed about Mr. Thomas Hutchinson.

Now, she knew no more about him, but she was beginning to realize how much she didn't know about him.

Now, too, she felt wretchedly guilty for being so immensely attracted to Mr. Hutchinson's closest friend. Though it was really quite silly for her to feel guilty for an unfulfilled flirtation. It wasn't as if a handsome peer of the realm like Lord Montague would ever take notice of a woman like Lucy.

Even so, her acquaintance with Lord Montague had had a profound effect on Lucy's engagement to Mr. Hutchinson. She had come to realize that Mr. Hutchinson might not be the right man for her. In less than a week she had discovered what she'd been unable to discover in the past six years. She ought to be thankful for that, but she wasn't.

She most fervently prayed that Mr. Hutchinson had not met with any misfortune, but if he were still alive and unharmed, she would feel duty bound to continue on with plans to marry the man. She would, however, give him the choice of a swift marriage or of calling it off entirely. Her ultimatum. His choice. She smiled as she thought of Hannah's *ultimatey.*

With deep disappointment, she eyed Lord Montague as he dejectedly trudged back to the coach. Her worry mounted.

"Come, let's get you something to eat," he said, striving for cheer as he came to sit opposite her.

She nodded solemnly. Her nausea was less today. She suspected it was because her stomach was as empty as a church at midnight. "So Mr. Hutchinson still has not come home?"

"That's right."

A moment later, his coach pulled to a stop in front of Devere House. "You must join me for dinner, my lord." She had sent a messenger ahead to announce her return to Devere's servants.

He shook his head. "Now that we're back in London, we must be cognizant of your sterling reputation. It wouldn't do for you to be entertaining a man like me without the benefit of a chaperone."

She attempted to mask her disappointment. He was tying her hands so she could not have a part in finding her missing fiancé. "Then we'll discuss this further in your coach."

He stiffened. "You'll eat first."

She dared not argue further. His clipped tone told her he would not tolerate her dictating to him. "Excellent," she said with false bravado. "When, my lord, will you and I be able to discuss our mutual quest?"

Even though dusk had fallen, she could clearly read the perplexed look on his lordship's face. The cleft in his chin dimpled even more deeply.

"Will it appease Miss Lucy Beresford if I give you my word to pay a call at Devere House tomorrow afternoon after I've spoken with the Foreign Secretary?"

"That is exactly what will please me, my lord. It's very kind of you to be mindful of my claim to your friend. I think you cannot refute that I have every right to be involved in the search for him."

"We shall see, Miss Beresford. We shall see."

THE FOLLOWING AFTERNOON, Monty made his way to Whitehall and to Lord Stewart's office. Lord Stewart, who was the same age as and a close friend of Monty's late father, had been active in the diplomatic corps since he was a young man and had been Foreign Secretary for the past two years. Because of his father's relationship with Lord Stewart since their days at Oxford, Monty had known him all his life.

Though he was in his sixties, Lord Stewart seemed younger, perhaps because he was still possessed of thick, dark hair and tended toward the slender side. He stood and greeted Monty amiably when Monty entered the large chamber, which was brightened by a bank of tall windows that looked out over the busy River Thames a short distance away. At least the river's customary foghorns would not be disturbing them today. It was a rare day when London skies were as clear and blue as they were on this day.

"Please sit," Lord Stewart instructed.

Both men sat and stared at one another for a moment. Before Monty could address the purpose of his visit, the Foreign Secretary said, "I've been expecting you."

Dread crept through Monty. As difficult as it was for him to articulate, he finally said, "Please don't tell me Hutchinson's dead."

Lord Stewart drew in a long breath. "The fact is, we don't know. He is, indeed, missing."

"That's bloody obvious! The man's been gone almost two weeks."

"I know how close you and Hutchinson are." Lord Stewart pursed his lips and looked as if he were deep in contemplation. "Because of that, I'm willing to share with you the facts as we know them—and they are few. You will appreciate that this is not information that is to be shared."

The first thing Monty thought of was Miss Beresford. She had every right to be apprised of the situation involving her betrothed. Though he didn't know her well, Monty believed Miss Beresford could be trusted to keep confidences. She might be as delicate as a butterfly's wings, but that delicacy was deceptive. No other women he knew could converse so intelligently about matters of government. And unlike most other women, she had no interest in gossip. She had even managed to spend four full days in his company without ever once bringing up the matter of her wardrobe, though from the quality of her dress, he knew she must care deeply about clothing. In so many ways, she was unlike most women he knew, even his beloved sisters.

But the Foreign Secretary was not expected to know Miss Beresford could be trusted with confidential information. Monty wanted to plead for her but instead answered Lord Stewart with a barely discernable nod.

"Only because of your father and the fact I've known you since you were in the cradle, will I tell you everything I know. Allow me to start at the beginning." He sat back and steepled his fingers while regarding Monty. "About six weeks ago, an army officer who was highly valued by Wellington died."

"In London?"

"No. He was making his way to London from France but died in Dover. Murdered. He'd been desperate to get to London to sound a warning."

Monty's brows hiked.

"The soldier—his name was Lieutenant Harmon—used his dying breath to impart to a fellow soldier the nature of his mission to London."

"This Harmon . . . was he a spy?"

Lord Stewart nodded. "Thank God Harmon trusted the other soldier to carry on with the message, or else we'd still be in the dark."

Monty frowned. "And we'd still have Hutchinson."

The Foreign Secretary winced. "True."

"So what was this vital message?"

"A nobleman was to carry out the assassination of a high-ranking British official."

"That's it? You don't know the name of the nobleman, nor the name of the man being targeted for assassination?"

"That's correct."

"With whom did you share this information?"

"Thomas Hutchinson."

"No one else?" Monty was incredulous.

"No one."

"How in the devil was Hutchinson supposed to operate from such sketchy nothingness?"

Lord Stewart shrugged. "I passed the little I knew on to him because he ranks fairly high in Society. He's welcomed at both Brook's and White's. I believe he had the social aplomb to extract further information."

"All by himself? You wished to pit him against an assassin? I doubt I could have succeeded, but I wish to God you'd have let him enlist me—and others—with the assignment." If he had, Hutchinson might still be with them.

The Foreign Secretary's voice was grim when he said, "If only hindsight were foresight."

Monty glared. "Hindsight has nothing to do with my anger. You pushed my closest friend—who's basically a clerical worker—into the sights of an apparently seasoned assassination."

"I know. I've chided myself a thousand times since Hutchinson has gone missing. I realize now it was not a one-man mission."

"Was Hutchinson keeping you abreast of his investigation?"

Stewart sighed. "There hadn't been much to share."

Were Monty involved in this clandestine inquiry, he knew very well the first thing he would do. "Were you able to connect Hutchinson with the soldier who was the recipient of Harmon's last words?"

Lord Stewart smiled. "You and your friend think alike. That's the first thing Thomas Hutchinson asked for."

"I should like the same information."

"Then you plan to take up where your friend left off?"

"I intend to find my friend. That's all. Let your soldiers thwart assassination attempts."

"You, my dear lord, are well equipped to thwart assassinations. Are you not reputed to be one of the finest swordsmen in all of London?"

"Fighting for one's life is considerably different than fencing at Angelo's studio on Piccadilly." He glared some more at what he now considered to be the inept Foreign Secretary. "I may be a patriot, but I'm not a fool."

"If you're to be looking for Hutchinson, you must be ready to defend yourself against sinister forces."

Perhaps Monty would not share with Miss Beresford these things he had learned today. He had no right to jeopardize her life. Given her small size, she would be at a significant disadvantage to ever defend herself against sinister forces.

"Give me the name of the last man with whom Harmon spoke."

The Foreign Secretary opened up a desk drawer and began to shuffle through some papers. Several moments later, he said, "Here it is." He unfolded a sheet of paper and squinted at the writing. "His name is Albert Thomas. He's presently attached to the Horse Guards."

Monty had no need to write down the name. He was blessed with a good memory. "Please consider my next question seriously." He paused, his eyes boring into the other man's. "Can you tell me anything else—any line of inquiry—Hutchinson may have asked you about?"

"I have asked myself the same question hundreds of times now, and the answer is always the same. Nothing else."

"And since he's gone missing, have you or the army put anyone else on this inquiry?"

Lord Stewart pressed his thin lips together. "No."

"So my friend may be in grave danger, and you didn't have the decency to even try to extricate him?"

"Of course I wanted to, but we have nothing to point us in any direction."

Monty stood. Were Lord Stewart not a lifelong friend of his father, Monty would like to have crashed a fist into the man's face. Stewart got Hutchinson into a possibly life-threatening situation but couldn't lift a finger to help him out of it. "I mean to find my friend."

With those parting words, Monty turned on his heel and stormed from the Foreign Secretary's huge, sunlit chamber.

With a lump lodged in his throat, Monty thought of his friend. He hoped to God Hutch was somewhere he could see the sunshine.

>>>>><<<<<

HAD HE NOT given Miss Beresford his word that he would come to her as soon as he spoke to the Foreign Secretary, Monty would have gone straight to the Horse Guards to seek Albert Thomas. But if Monty told Miss Beresford he would call, then he intended to do exactly that.

As it was, he had misgivings about sharing what he'd learned with the lady. It was possible he could be putting her life in jeopardy, just as Hutch's was.

His gut tightened. *Please let my friend be alive.*

At the suitable time for paying morning calls, he rapped upon the door at Devere House, knowing full well Miss Beresford would not be entertaining any other callers until her cousin or cousins returned from Brighton.

A footman showed him in and led him upstairs to the drawing room. "I shall tell Miss Beresford that Lord Montague is calling."

Moments later, she strolled into the morning room wearing a flimsy dress that was neither blue nor green but an amalgam of the two. Her ginger-haired maid silently followed before taking her own seat in a sunny corner of the chamber where she began to peruse one of those periodicals women seemed to find so fascinating.

He still marveled at how youthful Miss Beresford looked, though he knew she must be at least three-and-twenty. Even her voice conveyed the youthfulness of a girl nearly a decade younger.

As she sat on the silken sofa which was the chamber's most prominent piece of seating, he had to remind himself that even though she looked like a fresh debutante, she was a mature woman who was exceedingly well informed and articulate. In addition, she had been a betrothed woman longer than most of his married acquaintances had been wed. He must stop thinking of Miss Lucy Beresford as a girl straight from the schoolroom.

She initiated the conversation, careful to keep her tones so low that her maid would not be able to make out the words. He wondered why she was so interested in secrecy.

"I would rather my maid not know about Mr. Hutchinson being missing. For the sake of these conversations, oblige me by referring to Mr. Hutchinson as . . . shall we say Lord Edgar?"

"If you like."

Her tone brightened. "I'm most grateful you've come to me straightaway from Whitehall."

"I wish I had more information to share."

Even the thought of what she was going to say next upset her thoroughly, she hoped she could approach the subject without bursting into tears. "Before I learn what you've discovered this day, I must tell you, my lord, that I had a rather clandestine meeting with Devere's young groom. I gave him permission to visit his brother. You'll remember his brother's the one who scavenges the River Thames. He's to find out if his brother knows of any bodies which might have been taken from the river in the past two weeks. I told him we need to know about things like hair color and quality of clothing." Her voice shook on that last sentence.

An incredibly sad look on his face, his lordship somberly nodded. "I'm praying he brings us no unwelcome news."

"As am I."

She attempted a smile. "Now as to your news. Was Lord Stewart able to confirm that . . . Lord Edgar was, indeed, involved in—" She dropped her voice again. "In spying?"

For the sake of furthering this confidential talk, Monty moved to sit beside her on the sofa. "Yes, that was confirmed," he said.

The lady's light rose scent was the perfect complement to a perfect spring day. Breathing in the essence of spring while sitting next to this utterly feminine creature lifted spirits dragged down by mounting worry over his friend.

What a pity that Hutch could not be enjoying this time with his own fiancée. What a fool Hutch had been not to see this lady's many fine attributes. What a pity beauty was not one of them.

"I beg that you share all you've learned."

"Would that there were more to share. Unfortunately, neither he nor Hutchinson knew much of anything." He proceeded to tell her the little bit he had learned from the Foreign Secretary.

Her brows lowered. He couldn't tell if she was angry or if she was deep in contemplation. Perhaps it was a bit of both.

"Do you mean to tell me all the information poor Mr. Hutchinson received was that—let me see if I got this correctly—*a high-ranking man is to assassinate a high-ranking Brit?*"

"That's the gist of it."

"It's the most useless piece of information imaginable."

"An accurate assessment."

"It makes no sense. We must speak to the man who conveyed the information from the dying—" She lowered her voice to a whisper. "Spy."

It was uncanny how much this woman's thoughts paralleled his own. Perhaps less than being uncanny, it was more that each of them possessed critical thinking skills. His sisters, who considered themselves bluestockings, would be mortified if he ever admitted that heretofore he'd not thought women capable of such skill. Miss Beresford kept destroying many of his preconceived notions about her gender.

"We?" he asked.

"Yes, we. I will not remain idle while the very life of . . . Lord Edgar is at stake. May I remind you that it's broad daylight, my maid will accompany us, and we shall be in the world's busiest city. Nothing will appear untoward. No one will dare question my respectability."

It was true that now they were back in the Capital, Miss Beresford's seeking to find her betrothed would arouse no censure.

He frowned. "I hope we're not putting too much hope in the man's memory, but it does seem he's the one with whom we need to start."

Her face brightened. "You found out how we could contact him?"

"You think you're the only one with an inquiring mind?" he chided good-naturedly.

She shrugged. "I am not accustomed to anyone thinking the same way I do."

He felt the same. Again. "His name is Albert Thomas, and we ought to be able to find him at the Horse Guards."

She eyed her maid and raised her voice. "Hannah. Could you please collect our hats and spencers? Lord Montague is going to carry us to the Horse Guards."

Chapter Ten

Lucy and her maid stood off to the side at the Horse Guards Parade while Lord Montague made inquiries about Albert Thomas. The soldiers, not donning their dress uniforms, were going through their everyday routines, but Lucy found their disciplined approach fascinating to watch.

"I never seen such well-trained horses," said Hannah, who was unable to remove her eyes from the maneuvers. "It's like someone put a magic spell on them."

"Not magic. Just hard work and a lot of repetition."

"Look at the size of the soldiers! I'd never be afraid if I had one of those men hovering about."

"I keep telling you, you've nothing to fear in the neighborhoods we frequent."

Hannah ran her gaze over her well-dressed mistress. "It's you who are too complicit. Anyone could look at you and tell yer rich. What's to keep some cut-throat from stealing yer jewels in broad daylight?"

"I believe you mean *complacent*, not *complicit*."

"You knew what I was talking about." The maid pouted. "Yer far too trusting."

It was a lovely day, and it always invigorated Lucy to be in London. Though she'd spent most of her life in the country, she preferred the excitement of the city and all it had to offer. Her gaze fanned to the broad, arched entryway where flanks of horses entered and exited the parade grounds. Lord Montague stood there and beckoned for her to join him.

She and Hannah made their way to his lordship as he began speaking with a soldier who looked scarcely old enough to be serving in the military.

"Miss Beresford," Lord Montague said, "may I present to you Mr. Albert Thomas? We've been given permission to speak with him privately in a room just down the corridor."

When they reached the room, Lucy asked her maid to stand near the door to make sure they would not be overheard. More than secrecy, though, Lucy sought to keep Hannah from learning the truth about Mr. Hutchinson. She and Hannah had always been honest with one another, but there were things Lucy would prefer her maid not learn. For as loyal as Hannah was, she lacked discretion. She loved to hear gossip. She loved to spread gossip. And she never met a piece of gossip she did not try to embellish.

"We wish to speak to you about Lieutenant Harmon's last words," Lord Montague began.

"Were you well acquainted with Lieutenant Harmon?" Lucy asked the youthful soldier.

He shook his head. "I'd never met him before those last moments."

"You knew he was dying?" Lord Montague asked.

He nodded somberly. "He told me he hadn't long."

"Please," Lucy said, "we want to hear exactly what happened to the best of your recollection."

"He was staggering off the boat there at Dover, and I looked from his uniform to the growing patch of bright red blood on his coat. I leapt toward him, told him I was a soldier, too, and asked if he needed help."

"This is important," his lordship said. "Try to recall as many of his words as you can."

Eyes heavenward, the soldier said, "He was having difficulty speaking plainly. He said I needed to deliver a message to Lord Stewart at the Foreign Office. I asked again if I could help him. His exact words were 'You can't. They've killed me.'"

They? "Did he say who *they* were?" she asked.

The soldier nodded. "The Frenchies. That's what he called them when I asked. I offered to go after them, but he said they'd already have caught another boat back to France, thinking he was already dead. By then he was having such trouble speaking that he pulled a letter from his jacket and pointed to the name—Lt. Godwin Harmon. His hand and voice were shaking. 'That's me,' he said. 'Tell Stewart a nobleman has come to London to assassinate someone very high up.'"

"Did he say who the nobleman was?" Lord Montague asked.

"No."

Has come? "Are you sure, Mr. Thomas, the dying man used the words *has come?*" she asked. That would imply that the assassin might not be from Great Britain. Or it could mean that an English traitor might be re-entering the country to carry out the dirty deed. Or it could even mean that the assassin was coming to London from the provinces.

Mr. Thomas nodded. "Those were his exact words, though the poor fellow was struggling powerfully to get them out."

Another line of inquiry occurred to Lucy. "Did you make any effort to secure his belongings?"

"I did. He had been struggling to carry his own gear. I thought if I was to deliver his message to the Foreign Secretary, I ought to bring his things as well."

Her gaze shifted from the soldier to the earl. "Did Lord Stewart mention that to you, my lord?"

Lord Montague did not look happy. "No."

"I believe we need to see the dead officer's possessions."

"Indeed we do." He looked at the soldier. "Do you have any more recollections?"

Mr. Thomas shook his head.

"Then I thank you for the information."

After Albert Thomas left, she turned to his lordship. "I must insist on accompanying you when you speak to Lord Stewart."

He drew a long breath of exasperation. "Of course you do, Miss Beresford." He did not sound pleased. "But everything Lord Stewart told me earlier was in confidence. He asked that I not tell anyone."

She was silent for a moment. "I'm grateful to you for including me, then. However, as Mr. Hutchinson's fiancée, I am entitled to know his fate. I should even be permitted to help in the quest to find him. And I intend to tell that to Lord Stewart."

Lord Montague would never be able to understand how difficult it was for Lucy to have uttered that last statement. She fully expected to be humiliated by his response. Nevertheless, she cocked her head, eyeing him, and continued. "Shall we go see Lord Stewart?"

That he put up no resistance pleased her.

As much as he wanted to refuse her request, Monty could not. She did have the right to try to find the man to whom she had been betrothed for six long years. She had even more of a right than he did. Her entire future was wrapped up with Hutch.

When they were shown into Lord Stewart's sunny office, Monty conducted the introductions.

"So you're Lord Devere's cousin?" the Foreign Secretary said to her.

"I am."

"Good man. For a Whig." Lord Stewart grinned. "Of course, I was closer to his father—and his father's brother, Richard Beresford.

Would that have been you father?"

Now she smiled. "Yes."

"Fine man. He was just a bit ahead of me at Oxford."

"Thank you. He was a fine man. In fact, he fairly well handpicked Mr. Hutchinson for my future husband. That's why I'm here. You see, I'm to marry Mr. Hutchinson. It is my intention to do everything in my power to find him."

Lord Stewart's gaze shifted from her to Lord Montague. "Ah, so that's why you've brought the lady."

"The lady's a great deal more forceful than she looks."

"We won't take much of your time, my lord," Miss Beresford said. "We merely want to look through Lieutenant Harmon's things."

He eyed her companion. "I completely forgot about those, though I daresay you will find nothing helpful there."

"I'm sure you're right, my lord," she said, "but please indulge us. I'm so distraught about poor Mr. Hutchinson."

It was all Monty could do not to laugh. Now the Chameleon was reverting to her delicate damsel persona.

The Foreign Secretary rang a bell, and seconds later a young man dressed in exceedingly fashionable attire entered from an outer office.

"Be a good chap and locate those personal effects of the deceased Lieutenant Harmon," Lord Stewart told the man.

The other man's face fell. "I've sent them to his family."

Lord Stewart faced his visitors and shook his head.

"I must see them." Miss Beresford said, then turned to Lord Stewart's secretary. "Do me the goodness to give me the address of where you sent Lieutenant Harmon's belongings."

The secretary held up an index finger. "It just may be possible that they've not yet been collected. The first place we sent them was not correct—my error. I inadvertently gave the direction of East Sussex rather than West Sussex. Allow me to look into it. It won't take but a minute."

Moments later, he reentered the chamber carrying a battered valise. "Success!"

Once the secretary had left them, Monty placed the valise upon a large writing table, unfastened it, and began to ruffle through its contents. "One would think we'd find his formal uniform here," he said, puzzled.

"Not necessarily. Remember, as an officer, he was likely a man of some means. Would he not have a servant to look after his dress uniform?"

He met her gaze and smiled. "I expect you're correct." It was really quite remarkable how dramatically she'd reversed from extreme shyness to assert herself so authoritatively.

"But . . . would an officer not have his servant accompany him on the packet to Dover?" she asked, eyeing the Foreign Secretary.

"A good observation, Miss Beresford," Lord Stewart said. "I asked the same question about his batman. It took some time to locate him. Apparently Lieutenant Harmon got the last spot on the Dover packet. Since then, his batman has returned to England and was at a bit of a loss without his master. But he confirmed that Harmon did not take a dress uniform. And when I questioned the man about his master's mission, he knew no more than Lieutenant Harmon had shared with me." The Foreign Secretary eyed the door. "I have a meeting to attend now. Feel free to stay here and look over the contents. You are, of course, at liberty to take anything you may need for the investigation, but do let my secretary know what item or items that might be."

Monty continued to fumble through the contents of the dead lieutenant's bag. There was precious little here to indicate much about the man Harmon had been. Most of the items—a change of stockings, a quill, a pouch half full of British and French coins, a chamber lock— could have belonged to anyone in any manner of professions. The only truly personal possessions were papers bound together with violet ribbon.

"Oh, dear," she said, "I don't feel right looking at his personal correspondence. That ribbon tells me those are love letters."

"Or they're meant to be disguised as love letters. I wish I knew more about cyphers and secret codes."

"Do you not think Lord Stewart would already have examined them for that?"

He handed the correspondence to her. "Allow me to ask Lord Stewart's secretary if he knows the answer to that."

The Foreign Secretary's man confirmed that a cypher expert had looked over the correspondence and was satisfied there were no important documents in the lot.

"As beastly as it will make me feel to probe the man's intimate contacts, we must ascertain if there's anything here to aid in our quest." She untied the riband and began to shuffle through the correspondence. It appeared half was from the dead man's mother in West Sussex and the other half from a Miss Elizabeth Cook in Surrey.

Miss Beresford handed the correspondence from the mother to Lord Montague while she moved closer to the window to begin perusing the other letters.

⟫⟪

LUCY QUICKLY SURMISED that Lieutenant Harmon was betrothed to Elizabeth Cook. Her letters were full of well wishes for his safety and hopes for their future together. Because Elizabeth Cook had dated her letters, Lucy was able to determine which was the most recent and eagerly read it.

My Dear Lieutenant Harmon,

It is with the greatest excitement imaginable that I received your last letter in which you disclosed your intention of selling your commission and coming home at the completion of your current mission. I know, my dearest, you are not at liberty to reveal the nature of your mission, but I am aware of how very important you are to our government and am enormously honored to call myself the future wife of Lieutenant Godwin Harmon. Soon now we'll be inhabiting our own little cottage and launching our life together. Imagine my excitement when I learned I would be able to see you in London in March!

As you requested, I quizzed my cousin regarding new Persons of Importance who've been inaugural attendees at Almack's. I told her I could not tell her why I needed to know but that it was very important that she not leave out anyone—male or female. She left off (as I instructed) this year's crop of debutantes but enumerated Viscount Fairfax, an older spinster from York named Miss Anabelle Simpson, Count von Gustafsen, Madame Bergier, Lord Bosworth, Monsieur Clavette, and Monsieur Allard. According to my cousin, the French persons were formerly at Louis XVI's Court before the revolution and have only recently made their way to England from Switzerland. She said it's still early days for a full crush at Almack's. More are expected as spring turns to summer.

I press your letters to my breast and await the day in the near future when we shall see each other.

Your fortunate lady,
Elizabeth

LUCY BURST INTO tears when she read the last. March was almost spent. Miss Cook would never see her lieutenant, never live in that little cottage, never experience that happiness that was so close to her grasp when she wrote the letter.

Lord Montague rushed to her. "What's the matter?"

She lifted her anguished face to his. "The poor lady! She was so happy at this writing." She shook her head woefully. "And none of her happiness was to come to fruition. Only vast sorrow." She handed him the letter.

As he took it, his arm snaked around her, his hand clasping her shoulder affectionately, his thumb etching sultry circles. "It is sad.

Hopefully, one day we'll be at liberty to tell her and his family that their heroic Lieutenant Harmon sacrificed his life for his country." He withdrew a handkerchief and dabbed at the tears sliding down her cheek.

As keenly as she felt Lieutenant Harmon's tragic death, she also began to experience a bubbling feeling at the intimacy of his lordship's touch. Never had she ever been so close to a man. True, Mr. Hutchinson, on the day of his offer, had pecked her mouth with his, but no other part of their bodies had touched. Mr. Hutchinson's quick peck was but a droplet of rain to the depths of the mountain spring of Lord Montague's tenderness.

But this was not the time to let her mind stray in that direction. It was far more important to determine if there might be a clue in this letter, a clue which would help lead them to a person who might be responsible for Mr. Hutchinson's disappearance. "It does seem to me—" sniff, sniff "—that this last letter has some information which could be most useful to us. You will note how recently it was written."

She looked up at him. Lord Montague was a tall fellow, to be sure. She felt even smaller than normal as she stood there. "Do you know any of those Almack's newcomers?"

He shrugged. "I wouldn't say I know them, but I know who some of the gentlemen are. Just vaguely."

"From Almack's?"

"Hardly. I saw the two Frenchmen one night at White's but did not actually meet them."

"Was Mr. Hutchinson with you?"

"I really can't remember. More often than not, the two of us are together."

"Do you recall if you were introduced to the French men?"

"Actually, now that I'm remembering the night, I'm fairly certain Hutch wasn't there."

"How do you remember?"

"Because we heard the men speak in French, and I remember thinking that Hutch would be lost. He speaks French very poorly."

She hadn't known that about her betrothed. French had always been spoken at her family's dinner table. Indeed, it was spoken in most homes of noble families.

"Who were you with that night?" she asked.

"I wasn't really with anyone, though I sat with Whiteside."

"Is he a Whig?" She was well aware that her cousin Devere and other prominent Whigs gathered at Brook's, not White's.

"Not that I know of. Lord Whiteside doesn't seem to be political at all. He is just as comfortable at White's as he is at Brook's. I can say with certainty that he's never taken his seat in the House of Lords."

"Did you not say my dear Mr. Hutchinson also holds membership at both clubs, White's and Brook's?"

"He does. I do, too."

"Have those two Frenchmen also been to Brook's?"

"I haven't seen them there, but I haven't been there much in recent weeks."

"Do you not think, my lord, that this may be a promising lead?" she asked.

"Because they're French?"

"Yes. And perhaps something as well-planned as an assassination attempt might just call for the services of two men, rather than a lone . . . Evildoer."

He looked at the letter again, memorizing the names of Almack's newcomers. "I've never heard of any of the women."

"Because my lord does not grace Almack's. What of the count? Do you know him?"

"I know of him. I believe he's a powerful man. I saw him at a rout at Lady Jersey's—he was speaking to the Duke of York."

The Regent's favorite brother. "Oh, dear, he certainly has ingratiated himself at the highest levels. What country does the count come from?"

"I think he's a Swede."

"Then one would hardly expect him to owe any allegiance to Napoleon."

"True."

"What about the Brits mentioned here? Do you know Lords Fairfax or Bosworth?"

He shrugged. "I know they're not new to London. Bosworth occasionally takes his seat in the House of Lords, and Fairfax was coming into Eton as Hutch and I were leaving."

"Then I doubt they'd be worth investigating. I wonder if the new people on Miss Cook's cousin's list have become regulars at Almack's."

"There is one way to find out, but I don't see how you can attend without a chaperone."

She cocked her head and eyed him with a mischievous grin.

"I don't trust that look in Miss Beresford's beautiful blue eyes."

"Do you not, my lord, have a married sister living here in London?"

He sighed. "Is there anything you don't know about me?"

"I'm sure there are many things I don't know."

"I suppose you would like me to encourage my sister to procure a voucher for you and to take you to King Street on Wednesday night?"

"Take *us* to King Street," Lucy corrected.

He glared. "Very well, Chameleon."

Chapter Eleven

Come Wednesday night, in the most proper, respectable manner possible, Lord Montague and his sister conveyed Miss Lucy Beresford to Almack's. His lordship's coach had collected her at Devere House, where he effected the introduction to his married sister, Lady Carrington. The lady shared her brother's dark hair and eyes, and though the resemblance between the siblings was striking, nothing about Lady Carrington was masculine. She was remarkably pretty and dressed as impeccably as her brother.

Lucy remembered reading about the lady's success the year she was presented. It was the year before Lucy's own presentation, and the newspapers at the time were full of accounts of the popularity of Lord Montague's sister, Lady Sarah Lansbury.

In contrast to her brother, Lady Carrington was a chatterbox. She went into a long story about how she had procured their Almack's vouchers from Lady Sefton. "Of course, I am a subscriber," she pointed out. "In fact, I never miss an assembly during the Season."

Then it stood to reason, Lucy mused, Lady Carrington would be an excellent source for information about newcomers to that venerable institution on King Street. "Have you, perchance, encountered any men—or women—who are Almack's novices this Season?" Lucy asked.

Lord Montague's flashing gaze met Lucy's. "Particularly foreigners?"

"I have met Madame Bergier there this Season. I can't think why she hadn't been to Almack's before. I daresay she's been living on Cavendish Square since we were children, Arthur. And she dresses divinely. She's a widow, you know. Very charming. She fled Paris during the Terror. Her husband didn't make it, but they apparently managed to divert their fortune to England."

It seemed odd to Lucy to hear his lordship addressed as Arthur since his closest friends called him Monty. But his sisters' acquaintance with him obviously predated the time of his succession to the Montague title, and he would always have been Arthur to them.

Even though Lucy had never believed the assassin would be a woman, Lady Carrington's information all but stripped Madame Bergier from their list of possible assassins. The dead man said that the assassin *has come to London*. Such an assertion removed from suspicion anyone who was already a long-time resident of London. Or at least it would seem so.

His lordship finally managed to break into his sister's soliloquy on Madame Bergier. "Have you met any of the lady's countrymen? Particularly any new to London?"

"I must confess, Arthur, I pay no heed to the men. Unless they're on the hunt for a wife of the *ton*, the men tend to confine themselves to the card room, and as you know, I abhor gaming of any kind. I'm always remarking to Carrington that he simply should not play for high stakes. I've seen too many noble families lose everything that's not entailed over the roll of dice or the turn of a card."

Lucy cut in. "What about any Frenchmen who appear to be wanting to mingle in Society?"

Lady Carrington thought for a moment. "A Monsieur Allard did ask me to stand up with him. Madame Bergier had introduced us. I refused to dance with him, of course. I am not on the Marriage Mart, and I do not wish to engage in flirtations. I go to Almack's to ogle the fashions and to associate with my female friends."

"Does this Monsieur Allard dance much?" Lord Montague asked. "Does it seem he's in the market for a bride?"

"He does dance a great deal but rarely with the same woman more than once. It's almost as if he's merely trying to make the acquaintance with as many well-connected Englishmen and women as possible. One sees him simply everywhere."

Lord Montague directed a significant glance at Lucy.

"To your knowledge, does Monsieur Allard associate with other Frenchmen?" Lucy asked.

"He seems to be in the company of Monsieur Clavette a great deal of the time. Monsieur Clavette is exceedingly quiet. In fact, I've wondered if he's deficient in English." She turned to her brother. "Pray, Arthur, why are you so interested in these French people?"

Before he could answer, the Montague coach came to a stop in front of Almack's, and the coachman opened the door and let down the steps.

During the year of her come-out, Lucy had spent a great deal of time at Almack's, but she never had the good fortune of attracting a husband. Fearing his plain daughter would be a hopeless spinster, her father had arranged the nuptials between her and Mr. Hutchinson. Since then, she had visited Almack's only sporadically during visits with her Beresford cousins.

For reasons completely different from Lord Montague's, Lucy loathed attending these assemblies. One as attractive and titled as his lordship would never understand the embarrassment one like Lucy experienced when, feet tucked under her skirts, hands clasped in her lap as she sat watching the dancers, man after eligible man filed past her and nary a one of them ever asked her to dance—with the exception of her kindhearted cousin, Lord Devere.

She had, thankfully, not come to Almack's to dance tonight. She and Lord Montague were on a mission.

Upon entering the ballroom, which was already crowded, the threesome stood near the doorway and surveyed the gathering. Lucy quickly estimated there were at least four hundred in attendance, with only about a fourth of them engaged in dancing.

Lord Montague spoke to his sister. "Do you see the Frenchmen?"

Her gaze trailed from the left side of the chamber to right, and she shook her head. "Really, Arthur, why this intense interest in Frenchmen?"

Lucy freed him from having to respond. "Perhaps, my lord, you should look in the card room."

"That's a good suggestion." He offered his arm to his sister, who glided with him along the perimeter of the dance floor. The elegant train of her flowing cream and gold gown added to Lady Carrington's regal bearing. Following them, Lucy felt like a mongrel trying to run with purebloods.

At the doorway of the cardroom, Lord Montague and his sister surveyed those seated at tables playing whist, Faro, and piquet. Her ladyship rammed her elbow into her brother's side. "That's Monsieur Clavette in the fuchsia waistcoat, and next to him, the one with the longish sand-colored hair, is Monsieur Allard."

Lord Montague nodded. "I believe I fancy a game of whist. You ladies may return to the ballroom."

Though Lucy had no interest in gambling, she had even less desire to establish herself in the familiar spot of a wallflower. Sighing, she followed Lady Carrington back to the ballroom. Her ladyship introduced Lucy to her circle of friends, though it was difficult to hear the ladies' voices over the drone of conversations and the orchestra music.

※

MONTY WAS WELL acquainted with one of the men at the table with the Frenchmen. Lord Burrell, who was the same age as Monty, was one of the leading Tories in the House of Lords. He and Monty were congenial to one another, even though they were on opposite benches in Parliament.

Lord Burrell looked up, smiled, and greeted Monty. "What a surprise to see you at Almack's, Lord Montague. Did you come for the cards?"

"As a matter of fact, I have."

"Allow me to make you known to my companions." Lord Burrell proceeded to introduce Monty to the two Frenchmen. He already was acquainted with the fourth player, Mr. Parish.

Monsieur Clavette was the quieter of the two Frenchmen. He appeared to take his gaming seriously. Monsieur Allard, on the other hand, laid down his cards and gave Monty his complete attention. "Ah, Lord Montague, I've read about your leadership in the House of Lords."

"I would not refer to my minor role as leadership." Monty eyed Burrell. "Lord Burrell, after all, is a member of the ruling party." And, as a leading Tory, Burrell had the ear of the Regent.

It was obvious to Monty that one who wanted to become acquainted with those at the higher levels of English government would do well to cultivate the friendship of Lord Burrell. Could Allard be the one sent to London to assassinate a high-ranking British official? Was Clavette his associate? Were both men sent here to kill?

"My dear Montague," Lord Burrell said, "after this hand, you may take my place and partner Parish. I promised a dance with Lady Burrell, and I don't mind admitting that I'm very much intimated by my bride. One does not want to ever cross her ladyship," he added with a chuckle.

Monty could well believe it. Lady Burrell, the former Susan Parker, had been friends with his sister Sarah, but the former Miss Parker's propensity to demand compliance with her every demand had soured the friendship.

The hand was soon completed, with Burrell and Parish losing. Monty shook Burrell's hand. "I'll have to do my best to dig us out of the hole you put us in," Monty teased as he took his seat with a Frenchman on either side and his partner, Mr. Parish, across the table.

As the cards were being shuffled, Monty turned to Allard. "How is it we've not met before, though I believe I've seen you at either White's or Brook's? Are you new in London?"

Allard shrugged his shoulders. "I came during the winter."

"From where?"

"Though I'm French, I've been living in Switzerland since that so-called Emperor destroyed the France I knew."

Monty nodded, turning to Clavette. "And what about you, monsieur?"

"Me? I, too, came via Switzerland." Clavette tossed a glance at his fellow countryman. "For the same reasons as my friend Allard."

Monty was dealt a strong trump, won the bid, and managed to win his first hand.

"I have not seen you at White's," Allard said to Monty.

"But, my dear fellow, my party is in opposition. Therefore, Brook's is the club where I spend most of my time. Do you have White's membership yourself, or do you come as a guest of a member?"

"I am fortunate to have made friends with men who invite me to that fine establishment on St. James."

Many of those from upper class French families lost everything, Monty knew. He suspected neither Allard nor Clavette possessed much wealth. "If you don't mind stooping down to the party that's not in favor, I would be happy to bring you to Brook's sometime as my guest."

Monsieur Allard smiled. "Would tomorrow be too soon?"

"Tomorrow would be perfect," Monty answered. It could not be sheer coincidence that this Frenchman and his friend were doing everything they could to assimilate into British Society. Not just assimilate. From what he'd heard of the man from his sister and seen himself, Allard's focus was clearly on cultivating friendships with those of the highest ranks.

Is that not what Harmon had spent his dying breath warning of? The assassin would be doing everything he could to become accepted at the pinnacle of English government. And though Monty had denied his own importance in the House of Lords, he was one of the most influential Whigs, though he wasn't nearly as powerful as Rockingham, who'd so recently married the youngest Beresford sister—that is, Devere's youngest sister, Miss Lucy Beresford's cousin. Devere himself was a powerful Whig, but Monty remembered that Lady Harriett Beresford and her new husband, Lord Rockingham, were spending their wedding trip at the Prince Regent's Royal Pavilion in Brighton.

Could Allard know Monty was close to Lucy Beresford? Perhaps he wanted to use Monty to get close to the lady's powerful relations.

Or perhaps they knew she was betrothed to Hutch. His gut plummeted. They might believe Hutch had shared his suspicions with her. In which case, she could be in danger.

For now, that supposition was all Monty had to go on.

WHEN HER FRIENDS became engaged in a conversation that did not include her, Lady Carrington turned to Lucy. "I must tell you, I got my hopes up when Arthur asked me to procure vouchers for him and a lady tonight."

"Why?"

"Because, my dear lady, never before has Arthur wanted to come to Almack's, much less to bring a lady. I was sure you were The One. After all, it's time he settled down. He is now thirty, you know. It's past time for him to start a family and secure the succession." The earl's sister sighed. "But, alas, he pays you not the slightest attention. Can you credit it? He takes the unprecedented step of actually escorting a lady to Almack's, then proceeds to abandon her to a stranger—though I assure you, my dear Miss Beresford, I do not in the least consider you a stranger, seeing that I am such excessively good friends with your lovely cousins. I feel as if we've known each other simply for decades. By the way, how old are you? I seem to think you came out some time ago, yet you have such a frightfully youthful countenance. Perhaps it's your petite size, or perhaps it's your singularly juvenile voice."

Lucy was unable to determine if she had just been complimented or criticized. "You have it wrong, my lady. I am betrothed to Mr. Hutchinson."

"Ah, that accounts for it! That also explains your dissimilarity to any woman with whom Arthur has ever been . . . involved."

Lucy's curiosity to know just what qualities Lord Montague would be attracted to in a woman was almost as strong as her desire to undercover the assassin. "I am well aware that I could never attract someone like Lord Montague."

"Oh, my dear lady, I did not mean that at all."

"I suppose all the women ever linked with your brother are exceedingly beautiful."

"That is true, but none of them ever seem to have conquered his heart. I was so hoping you would be The One. A connection with the Beresford family is one that is to be desired, after all."

A man in his fifties who was tall, slender, and possessed of a large, beak-like nose and thinning light brown hair threaded with gray came up to Lady Carrington and sketched a bow. "My dear Lady Carrington, was that gentleman who escorted you here tonight your fortunate husband? I have not had the pleasure of meeting him before." The man spoke with some kind of Scandinavian accent.

The lady giggled and fluttered her fan. "Dear me, no, Count. That was my brother, Lord Montague."

Count? And a Scandinavian accent? Could this man be the Count von Gustafsen mentioned by Elizabeth Cook in her letter to the dead Lieutenant Harmon? Lucy's attention turned to the man.

"Allow me to present to you, Count, my friend, Miss Lucy Beresford."

Lucy offered her hand, and the count placed a mock kiss just above her white glove. "You are related to Lord Devere?" he asked.

She nodded. "He's my cousin. In fact, I am staying at his house now, though he's away."

"I should be honored to meet him when he returns."

"You, sir, have the advantage on me," Lucy said. "You know my name, but I don't know yours."

He smiled down at her. "I am Count von Gustafsen"

"It is a pleasure to make your acquaintance." Lucy wholeheartedly meant those words. It looked as if she was going to get the opportunity to do some investigating herself.

"Since I know Lady Carrington never dances, I beg that you, Miss Beresford, will stand up with me."

She meant to be as charming as possible. "I would be honored."

As he led her onto the dance floor, he asked, "Are you new to London?"

"I have only just arrived, but I've been here at my cousin's many times. What of you, Count? You must have been here a long while to know so many people."

"Actually, I've only been here two months, but I enjoy meeting new people, especially the class of people one meets at a place like Almack's."

"Or White's?"

"There, too. I've been fortunate to have been invited there any number of times."

"My cousin, Lord Devere, prefers Brook's."

He nodded. "That's to be expected, given that he's so prominent a Whig."

"You know a lot about us."

"I find it interesting to keep up with those in the city in which I now reside. I've read often in the London newspapers about your cousin, Lord Devere, and his accomplishments in the House of Lords. You must be very proud of him."

"I'm proud of all my cousins."

"Your cousin, Harriett Beresford, recently married Lord Rockingham, did she not?"

"Indeed she did."

"I am told Lord Rockingham will one day lead the country. Is it true that he—and your cousin—are now guests of the Prince Regent in Brighton?"

"Yes, to my consternation. I had rushed to London to meet the Paragon who captured my beautiful cousin's heart, but I was too late. And to make matters worse—and lonelier for me—the Regent's invitation extended to my cousin Devere and his bride, who I was also anxious to meet. So both my cousins and their new spouses are away from London."

Then they took their places in the longway where there was no further opportunity to converse. At the completion of the set, he returned her to Lady Carrington, but before the count left them, his attention returned to Lucy. "Would you permit me to call upon you?"

"Of course."

"I suppose Lord Devere lives at a fine address like Grosvenor Square."

"Actually, Devere House is on Curzon. I find the address close to everything we enjoy most in London."

"What day do you accept callers?"

"I've only just arrived in London and haven't called on anyone yet or been called upon."

"Then I shall hope to catch you at home."

A moment after the count left, Lord Montague returned from the card room and asked Lucy to stand up with him. "I've taken the liberty of seeking permission from Princess Lieven to waltz with you." Her heart pounded. So this was to be a waltz! When she heard the orchestra begin, her heartbeat stampeded. Though she had practiced the waltz any number of times only with her dancing master, this would be the first time she had actually performed the waltz with a man.

When he drew her into his arms, her breathing became erratic. This closeness was incredibly intimate. He was so much taller, her head nestled close to his chest. His grip on her hand tightened. "I knew you were small, but I had no idea you were so very . . . little."

"Please don't liken me to a child. I am, after all, four-and-twenty years of age."

He tossed his head back and laughed. "I assure you, Miss Beresford, I do not think of you as a child." The pressure of his hand splayed on her back deepened.

Another tender gesture. A tingling sensation spread over her body. She had never before experienced anything like this. She could forget that an assassin was going to kill an important British official. She could forget that a soldier for the Crown had been ruthlessly murdered. She could even forget that she was betrothed to the best friend of the man in whose arms she was being held. All she could concentrate on was this moment of deep and total contentment.

Neither spoke for several moments. Then she had to mentally shake herself from this lulling pleasure. This dance with her meant nothing to Lord Montague—she was certain of it. He was merely being a gentleman.

Then he said something which shattered her composure.

Chapter Twelve

"Hutchinson's a fool not to have already wed you," Monty said. "There's something most alluring about one as delicate as Miss Lucy Beresford."

For the first time in his adult life, Monty had done something impetuous. More than a decade of schooling himself to carefully phrase his speech was blown apart after just a moment waltzing with the petite Miss Lucy Beresford. He had done the unthinkable: he had blurted out a compliment he had no right to give.

The delicate Miss Beresford was betrothed to Hutch! Hutch was Monty's closest friend and had been for most of their lives. Monty would never have thought himself capable of ever having designs on any man's wife or fiancée, much less that of his greatest friend. Not that he did, of course. He would never try to steal away his best friend's woman. In fact, he had never considered Miss Beresford in a romantic way.

Yet, his tongue had betrayed him, and he couldn't deny that his words accurately expressed his innermost thoughts. Hutch *was* a fool. And Miss Beresford was uncommonly feminine. If she were not engaged to his dearest friend, Monty might just find himself attracted to her.

But she was betrothed to Hutch.

Monty must force himself to look upon her in the same way he looked upon his sisters. The pity of it was, he did not think of her in the same way he thought of his siblings. If he could, then he would not desire to hold Miss Beresford close the way he held her right now. And she would not make him feel alive as he danced with her. Nor would he wonder what it would be like to press his lips against her. And he would certainly never want to whisk her into his arms and carry her off for lovemaking. But those uncommon feelings perfectly summed up the way Miss Beresford was affecting him tonight.

It must stop.

"I beg that you forgive me," he said. "If Hutch were here, I'd be asking his forgiveness for speaking to his betrothed with such impertinence."

He wondered if Miss Beresford was in love with Hutch. Hutch did hail from a family with noble connections. He had distinguished himself in the House of Commons. And Hutch was considered a fine-looking man. Any number of women had fallen in love with him since he'd left Oxford.

Monty shook himself inwardly. Of course, Miss Beresford must be in love with him. Otherwise, she would not be traipsing across England in a quest to find the man she was pledged to marry.

The Chameleon had reverted to her shy self. She made no response for several moments. Then she said, "Pray, don't berate yourself. I am unaccustomed to such flattery. Would that my fiancé spoke as prettily as you just did to me."

Poor girl. Hutchinson did treat her shabbily. "I am sure he will when he sees you again."

Why was it the longer Monty was with Miss Beresford, the lovelier she seemed? At least in his eyes.

He'd previously thought himself partial to lush women. The more pronounced the curves, the better. But those women no longer held such appeal—not since he had become acquainted with one whose every characteristic bespoke delicacy.

There was something about Miss Beresford that cried out to be caressed, carried, protected. She would probably be furious if she knew he was thinking that way about her right now. She did not in any way want to be treated like a child. He knew she was weary of being controlled by men. She was a woman of four-and-twenty who wanted to be the author of her own fate.

"When we can have privacy, we need to compare notes about the foreign men we've dealt with tonight," she said in a voice slightly louder than a whisper.

His step slowed, and he looked down at her pale head. "You mean you've made the acquaintance of a potential—let us use your term—Evildoer?"

"I have, with *potential* being the key word. And I'm anxious to hear what transpired with you and the Frenchmen."

"We will deliver my sister to Carrington House, then I'll have my coachman drive us around the streets of London while we share what we've learned tonight." He was still mightily determined not to enter the lady's lodgings at night without a chaperone. He must guard her reputation. For Hutch's sake.

"You dance well for one who claims to detest assemblies and balls," she said, her voice reverting to its normal tone. "I believe you get more practice than you own."

He chuckled. "It must be the skill of my partner." He spoke softly. "You're an excellent dancer."

She laughed. "I have a confession."

"What?"

"This is the first time I've ever waltzed. The year I came out, the waltz simply wasn't accepted in London, though my cousin Sophia assured me it was the rage on the Continent."

"Then dancing elegantly must come naturally to you." *Elegant.* The word did seem to describe her. Even her clothing—each dress he'd seen her wear—was elegant. Never again would he think Miss

Lucy Beresford plain.

When the dance ended, his disappointment surprised him. He'd never enjoyed dancing. Until tonight.

LATER THAT NIGHT, or more accurately, the next morning, his lordship's coach delivered his sister to her house on Manchester Square. Lucy had been a poor conversationalist on the drive there from Almack's. She was still immensely affected by Lord Montague's compliments. She was so unaccustomed to receiving praise that she wondered if such flattery was meaningless. Was there any sincerity in words issued by sought-after bachelors in the Capital to their dance partners? What a pity she knew so little of the ways of the *ton*.

After Lady Carrington disembarked from the coach, she turned back to face Lucy. "It has been a pleasure to make your acquaintance. May I call on you at Devere House? I frequently visit Lady Mary Luttrell, who also lives on Curzon Street."

"I would be delighted."

"I am only sorry you're betrothed to that rascal, Thomas Hutchinson. I had hoped my commitment-averse brother had found in you his perfect mate."

Lucy's heartbeat thundered. As attractive as she found Lord Montague, never would she have presumed that she was a fit match—a matrimonial match—for him! Even the fleeting contemplation of it accentuated her own feelings of inadequacy. A burning flush climbed up her cheeks.

Lord Montague chided his sister. "Really, Sarah, you're embarrassing poor Miss Beresford."

"Do forgive me, my dear lady, but I only speak the truth when I say I think you'd be perfect for my brother."

Once the coach door closed, his lordship sighed. "I do apologize for my sister's outspokenness. You'll understand why I could never trust her with a secret. She's incapable of discretion."

Lucy laughed. "Nevertheless, she's delightful. I must own I am exceedingly flattered over her acceptance of me. And I do understand why you don't share confidences with her. It's the same with me and my maid. I cherish her, but she loves to gossip."

He nodded. "I believe my sister would prefer a juicy piece of gossip over a new diamond bracelet. Speaking of gossip, what can you tell me?"

"I met the Swedish Count von Gustafsen. I even danced with him."

"Did you find out how long he's been here in London?"

"Just two months."

"That tallies with what Lieutenant Harmon said, wouldn't you say?"

"Yes."

"How promising."

"He wants to call on me."

"You're not to see him alone. The man could very well be a murderer."

"You would have me pretend not to be at home?"

"No, but as soon as your servants inform you he's waiting, you must send a note to me. No matter what I'm doing, I'll come. Please, give me your word."

"You have my word."

For the second time tonight, she was uncommonly flattered. Lord Montague worried about her welfare. His concern was especially comforting since she was currently so alone in London. How nice it was to have someone who cared, though she could hardly credit it.

A moment later, he asked, "How old would you say the count is?"

She contemplated the question for a moment. "Early to mid-fifties, I should imagine."

"Does that not seem quite old to be an assassin?"

"I'm no authority on assassins, having never previously met one," she said. "I will own, though, the count doesn't look very menacing."

"Did you have much opportunity to talk with him?"

"Just a few minutes, if that."

"Still, it's promising. What kind of questions did he ask?"

She thought back over the words they'd exchanged. "Actually, I think the only question I remember him asking is if he could call on me."

"Perhaps he's just a lonely man in a strange country." He shrugged. "Or perhaps he's looking for a suitable bride." His lordship's voice turned stern. "He's too old for you."

"More likely, he's just lonely. I cannot imagine living in a country that was not my own."

"Why is he here?"

"In so short a time, we had no opportunity to discuss that."

"We need to find out."

"Yes, we do."

"Did you learn anything about him?"

"I did. I learned that he's desirous of meeting Englishmen of high rank."

"Does that not sound like something Lieutenant Harmon warned of? An assassin who wanted to mingle with those of highest rank?"

"I would hardly call myself one of high rank. Why should he desire to cultivate my friendship?" she asked.

"Has it not occurred to you that he finds you desirable?"

"I can honestly say that has *not* occurred to me."

His lordship started to say something, then clamped shut his mouth. "What else can you tell me of him?"

"He seems to have learned who the important men are. He knew all about Devere's work in the House of Lords. He even knew my cousin's a Whig."

"How curious. He seems to have learned much in just two months."

"Indeed, he has. He's been to White's. He was desirous of meeting Lord Carrington. He even thought when you came into the ballroom with your sister that you must be her husband."

"Hmmm. Carrington's quite a powerful Tory."

"And you permitted your sister to marry a Tory?" she asked playfully.

"My brother-in-law's a fine man, in spite of it." He smiled. "And he has to be to put up with my sister, whose tongue never stops."

"Your sister *is* vastly different from you."

"None of us Lansburys are as talkative as Sarah. If our mother wasn't the angel she was, we would have suspected Sarah the product of . . . well, I needn't speak of such in front of a maiden."

A lover's child.

A moment later, she asked, "What of your Frenchmen? Did you have the opportunity to converse with either of them?"

"Enough. The quiet one rarely talks, but Monsieur Allard is congenial and inquisitive. In fact, he jumped at the invitation to be my guest at Brook's."

"That sounds far more suspicious than my poor count."

"*Your* count?" he asked with mirth.

"You know what I mean," she replied with an equal dose of levity. "Do you have any idea when you and Monsieur Allard will go to Brook's?"

"Tomorrow night. His idea."

She clapped her hands with glee. "We're getting closer to knowing what's happened to poor Mr. Hutchinson."

Of course, the fate of her betrothed might not be a source of happiness, but any progress toward finding him was encouraging. The longer he was gone, the more she feared for his life. "Do you have any plan to find out if the French man or men are the assassins?"

The coach was turning on to Curzon Street.

"None at all."

She understood. For now, it was a matter of listening and learning from the foreign men. Perhaps the Evildoer would reveal himself or themselves upon further contact.

When the coach came to a stop in front of Devere House, she was sorry. The lonely house held no allure.

"If the count calls tomorrow, notify me immediately," Lord Montague said when he walked her to the front door.

Chapter Thirteen

The very next morning as Cummings was tying Monty's cravat, a knock sounded upon his chamber door. "An urgent message for you, my lord," his footman said.

Before Cummings could so much as fetch the letter, Monty had already instructed the footman to race to the mews and order his saddlehorse to be brought around immediately. Even without reading the missive, Monty knew he was needed on Curzon Street.

He quickly opened the letter and read Miss Beresford's short message.

My Lord,

As you requested, I'm notifying you that Count von Gustafsen has called and awaits me in the drawing room. I won't go there until I'm notified that you've arrived.

Lucy Beresford

Ten minutes after Monty left his house, he had handed off his horse to an ostler and was knocking at the door of Devere House where the footman, upon being presented his card, immediately showed him to the drawing room.

An older man whose height equaled Monty's but who was much slimmer, stood and effected a courtly bow, and introductions were exchanged.

"I've not had the pleasure of actually meeting you before. You are a friend of Miss Beresford's?" Monty asked.

"I met her last night at Almack's."

"I must have missed you. I was in the card room."

"I don't indulge in the English pastime of gambling." The count shrugged. "My pockets are not as deep as yours, my lord."

How was this man privy to details about Monty's wealth? Monty had already wondered if the assassin's motivation for killing might be for money rather than politics. Count von Gustafsen could be a promising suspect in that regard, but if Monty were to wager, his money would be on one or both of the Frenchmen.

"Hello, gentlemen," Miss Beresford called from the doorway.

Both men turned to greet her, the count a little too enthusiastically to Monty's way of thinking.

As he watched Count von Gustafsen fawn over Miss Beresford, Monty tried to imagine how a man who was just meeting her for the first time might look upon the lady. It was difficult for him to evaluate her appearance with fresh eyes. He'd become too familiar with her, too attached to the lady, though not romantically, of course. His own first impression had been uninspiring, to be sure. But since then, everything about her had grown more impressive. The woman he'd thought void of beauty now captivated him with her delicacy and elegance. And the shy personality she'd first revealed had been peeled away to reveal a woman of intelligence and maturity.

As for Count von Gustafsen, he was either enchanted over her or, if he *were* the assassin, he had a strong motive to be cultivating her friendship. Monty meant to find out which was accurate.

Monty's eye trailed over her from the tip of her flaxen head and down the slight curves of her slender figure. The upper part of her pale green dress showed quite a bit of skin so pale and smooth it resembled white rose petals. This was the first time Monty had allowed himself to observe the soft roundness of her bosom.

He'd been wrong to think her lacking in feminine curvature.

She faced Monty. "You've met the count?"

"Indeed."

She went to the sofa and sat. "Please, gentlemen, sit wherever you like."

To Monty's consternation, the count came and sat on the sofa on Miss Beresford's right.

"So, my dear Miss Beresford," the count said, "have you received any correspondence from your pair of newly married cousins?"

"No, but I've not presumed to initiate any. They are not yet even aware I'm here. I would have felt like an interloper if I were to intrude on their stay with the Regent. After all, it's the Rockingham's wedding trip."

"So you've not spoken with Lady Harriett about foiling the plot against the Regent?"

"I know no more than what's been reported in the newspapers."

It occurred to Monty that the investigation undertaken by Devere's sister and the powerful Parliamentarian she'd wed was not altogether different from what he and Miss Beresford were doing. Yet the culprits could not possibly be the same, as the one who had orchestrated the threat against the Regent was not connected to any foreign power. The deranged man had acted on his own to implement his twisted acts of murder and attempted murder.

"Ah, but, quite naturally, now the Regent must owe your cousin and her new husband a great debt," the count said.

Miss Beresford spoke with mock outrage. "As well he should."

The count regarded Monty. "Is Lord Rockingham a member of the Regent's inner circle then?"

"The Regent is in his sixth decade—the same age as those he's closest to." Monty realized the count could almost be a contemporary of the regent. "I don't think Lord Rockingham has reached thirty yet."

She shrugged. "I'm not sure of Lord Rockingham's age, but he's a great friend of my cousin Devere, who is just past thirty."

"I see," the count said. He sounded disappointed.

Monty wondered if the count had befriended this lady under the misapprehension that, through her, he might have an *entrée* into the Regent's inner circle. Good lord, was the Regent the target of another bizarre plot?

The count recovered and turned his attention once again to Miss Beresford. "I haven't told you, Miss Beresford, how lovely you look today."

Now she returned to her bashful persona. "That's very kind of you to say."

Monty's hands fisted. What right did this man have to be complimenting her like that? Why had Monty himself failed to make a similar comment? Now that the other man had done so, Monty realized the count spoke the truth. She really did look lovely. It was good for her shaky confidence that a man was speaking so prettily to her, but it rankled Monty, who wasn't convinced the man was sincere. And if he were sincere?

Monty did not like him.

Miss Beresford's shy gaze flicked to Monty.

"It seems Count von Gustafsen and I are in complete agreement on your loveliness," he said, partly to bolster her confidence but mostly because it was true. As much as he disliked the count, they were in perfect agreement. "You look most fetching this afternoon." He wished he had been complimentary regarding her appearance the previous night when they went to Almack's.

Her lashes lowered as if she were contemplating her lap. "Thank you, my lord," she said in a voice barely above a whisper.

"I fail to understand why some fine young man hasn't won your heart," the count said to her.

"One has," Monty growled. "Miss Beresford is betrothed to my friend, Mr. Thomas Hutchinson."

The count didn't respond for a moment. Was he that disappointed? Then, finally, he turned to her. "Does this Mr. Hutchinson reside in London? I don't believe I've had the pleasure of meeting him."

"Yes, he does," Monty answered. They need not get into a discussion about Hutch's absence.

"I must own," the count said, "I am most disappointed to learn that you're already spoken for, my dear Miss Beresford."

Her gaze once again dropped to her lap.

"So, Count, what brings you to London?" Monty asked, only barely able to control his sudden anger.

"To be perfectly honest, I'm searching for a bride."

Wasn't the man awfully long in the tooth to be seeking matrimony at so advanced an age? How arrogant of him to think himself fit for a woman as young as Miss Beresford. Though Monty had to admire how thoroughly the man had researched those in English Society. The Beresfords were one of the oldest and most respected families in England. And also one of the wealthiest.

Monty glared at the Swede. "Then I daresay you must be gravely disappointed to learn of the existence of Mr. Hutchinson."

"Indeed I am."

"You men will put me to the blush! Pray, can we speak of something else?"

The count directed his attention to her. "I look forward to meeting the fortunate man who's won your hand."

Monty's mouth curved into a smile. "I will be happy to introduce you two myself." Again, he did not want to admit that Hutch was nowhere to be found. He hoped Miss Beresford understood and would keep silent about her fiancé.

"Tell me, my lord," the count said, "does Mr. Hutchinson serve in Parliament?"

Had the count not previously admitted to keeping abreast of all the English political news? Until a couple of weeks ago, Hutch was frequently mentioned in the newspaper accounts. He was always described as *a leading member of the Opposition*. As was Monty. "Yes, he does."

The count frowned. "I don't recall having read about him."

The man had to be lying. If he knew that Monty and Devere were leading Whigs, he was bound to have read about Hutch's Parliamentary exploits.

The count's attention returned to Miss Beresford. "Mr. Hutchinson is most fortunate to have won your heart."

It occurred to Monty that poor Miss Beresford had not won Hutch's heart. The fool. She deserved to be loved.

Her gaze reverted to her lap once again.

The case clock on the mantelpiece chimed the hour.

"Dear me," the count said. "I must be going."

At least the man possessed the good sense to stay just the right amount of time. Nothing was more annoying to a hostess than a tedious guest who refused to leave after pleasantries were exchanged.

>>><<<

"So, my lord, what are your impressions of Count von Gustafsen?" she asked once she was assured the visitor had left the house.

"They're not particularly favorable."

"Then you think he might be our assassin?"

"I think he's not an admirable man."

"And you base that opinion on what?"

"I cannot admire a man who blatantly admits he's in search of a wealthy wife."

"While he did say he'd come here to search for a wife," she said, "I don't recall him mentioning that she needed to be an heiress."

"It was implied. He admitted that his pockets were not as deep as mine, and he confessed that the attraction of Almack's was the privileged class of its attendees. The man's a fortune hunter. Nothing more, in my opinion."

She wondered if Lord Montague's grumpy mood had to do with him being summoned so early in the day. She had not seen him in this foul a temper since that morning she'd insisted on leaving Bath with him. And that morning she'd been fully aware of how displeased he was with what he viewed as her authoritarian demands.

"Allow me to play devil's advocate," she said. "If, perchance, the count were the assassin, would he not have to offer a plausible reason for having come to London?"

"Possibly."

"Do you not think wife hunting to be believable?"

His lordship's eyes narrowed. "The only way a woman as young and appealing as you would ever be interested in marrying a man like him would be if he were possessed of a fortune—which he freely admitted he did not have."

She was taken aback when he'd used the word *appealing* in connection with her. Could it be that familiarity had elevated his impression of her? The way he'd tossed out the remark came so naturally, she thought perhaps he might truly be sincere. Which, of course, softened her toward him all the more.

"But you must own, he's determined to ingratiate himself into the Society of those who move at the highest levels of government—not that that includes me, but it does include those I'm connected to. Even if they are Whigs," she said.

"True. It's the same with Monsieur Allard."

"And I think both bear our scrutiny, along with Monsieur Clavette."

He nodded. "You're right."

"What now?"

"Let's see what I learn tonight about our Frenchmen." He went to get up, but a footman came into the drawing room and addressed Miss

Beresford.

The footman looked perplexed. "Miss Beresford, I tried to tell the groom he could not have a private audience with you, but he insists."

Her gaze whipped to Lord Montague's. Her heart pounded. She prayed the groom wasn't going to tell her that Mr. Hutchinson's body had been found.

His lordship's face blanched as he nodded solemnly.

"Please show the groom in. Lord Montague and I wish to speak with him."

Chapter Fourteen

Dried mud on his boots, hat in hand, the young groom entered the drawing room, respectfully bowing his head as his gaze met Lucy's.

After presenting him to the earl, she asked, "You've spoken with your brother?"

"Indeed, miss."

She could not quell the shaking which started to overcome her body. She was terrified to learn that Mr. Hutchinson's body had been found in the murky waters of the River Thames. She was unable to force out words. Her agonized gaze shifted to his lordship.

He looked no more composed than she, but he did manage to speak. "Have . . . bodies been recovered from the river these past two weeks?"

"Aye, my lord. Just two, which me brother says is uncommonly few. He attributes the small number to the warmer weather. Says there's more fatalities in the winter."

"I would have thought it the other way around," Lord Montague said, concern still etched on his face.

The groom nodded. "One of the two bodies was a lady what had long brownish hair. Her clothing was said to indicate she was not from the Quality."

"And the man?" his lordship asked.

"He'd been in the water for more than a week. His clothes, except for his boots, were gone."

Her stomach dropped. Her voice shook when she asked, "What color was his hair?"

"'Twas black."

Relief swished over her. Thank God Mr. Hutchinson's hair was not black!

"You are sure his hair was black—not brown?" Lord Montague inquired.

The groom shrugged. "I didn't see him meself, but that's what my brother told me."

"Did he say how large a man the deceased was?" his lordship asked.

The groom nodded. "The dead man was about my size, according to my brother's account."

Lucy's gaze raked over the groom. He was considerably shorter than Lord Montague, and Mr. Hutchinson was tall like his friend. This revelation instantly swept away her gloom, though she was still shaky.

Lord Montague also looked relieved. He withdrew a coin from his purse and gave it to the groom. "We thank you for undertaking these inquiries."

After the groom left, the two investigators expressed their pleasure. "There's hope dear Mr. Hutchinson's alive," she exclaimed.

A smile barely lifted the corners of Lord Montague's mouth. "If only we were closer to knowing where he's gone."

"It's terribly frustrating. We know no more of his whereabouts than we did a week ago. And he'd already been gone a week then."

"Most likely we can rule out suicide."

"That at least is a comfort," Lucy conceded.

"So there are two explanations for his absence." Lord Montague held up his index finger. "One, he's been killed by the assassin because he learned his identity. Or—" he held up a second finger, "—he's being held against his will until the foul deed is done."

The assassination. She hugged her shivering arms. "Let us pray it's the latter."

"I should think the assassin would not be foolish enough to hold Hutch at his own lodgings."

"But it would still behoove us to look into the possibility."

"True," he said. "So we need to find out where the Frenchmen and the count live."

"Are you sure we should eliminate Lords Fairfax or Bosworth? Were they not the names mentioned in Lieutenant Harmon's letter? Perhaps we should find a way to search the peers' residences, too."

"For now, at least, I prefer to eliminate them."

She nodded. "I do find it difficult to credit that British aristocrats could be traitors to the Crown."

"An opinion I share."

"So once my partner-in-inquiry—that's you—learns the location of our... suspects... we must endeavor to determine if my fiancé is being kept prisoner at one of their residences."

―――

SHARING CONFIDENCES WITH and soliciting the opinion of a female was alien to Monty. No woman had ever before managed to insert herself and her ideas so thoroughly into his life. Now, he was taking it a step further by treating Miss Beresford as an equal partner in his efforts to find Hutch. How in the devil had this happened?

He had to admit the woman was possessed of an intelligence that could challenge most men he knew. For that, he was grateful. In the turmoil Hutch's loss had thrust him into, he also had to admit that it was oddly comforting to be able to share his grief and his worries with someone, to have another with whom to explore solutions. If there was a solution.

As the worrisome days stretched on, he had come to realize there was no one else he would rather count as his co-investigator than Miss Lucy Beresford. He'd gotten to where he couldn't imagine a day going by without seeing her. So later that afternoon, after a few quick inquiries, he hastened back to Devere House to share with her what he'd learned.

Her amazing eyes brightened when she greeted him in the sunny drawing room. "I knew you'd have no difficulty finding out their whereabouts, but even I am amazed at how quickly you've succeeded, my lord."

She'd been sitting on the sofa, reading, and when he entered the chamber she beckoned for him to come sit beside her. This was the second time she had dispensed with the practice of having her maid sit in the corner as a chaperone. Such proprieties really were no longer necessary, he admitted to himself. She was an unimpeachable lady, and, besides, their activities were not being subjected to the city's gossipmongers.

As soon as he sat by her, he was aware again of her faint scent of roses. It was the same fragrance his adored mother had always worn. "You may not be as appreciative when you hear what I've learned."

Her face fell. "Why?"

"The Frenchmen stay at modest lodgings on Piccadilly. I doubt there's a dungeon-type chamber there where Hutch could be held."

She nodded solemnly. "And the count?"

"That's a bit more promising. He's actually staying in a London house near the Melbournes' Thames-side mansion. He's leased the house for a year."

"The Frenchmen's lodgings lack promise, but I'm going to contrive a way to gain admission to the count's."

"You'll do no such thing! You're not to go near that man unless I'm present."

"Then what do you propose?"

"I'll think on it."

"As to the Frenchmen, what if I send my maid? I could have her dress as a housemaid—"

He cut her off. "I cannot favor anything that jeopardizes an innocent female."

"What if you sent your valet with her?"

A grin slowly spread across his face. "Are you trying to play Cupid?"

"All I'm trying to do is to find my fiancé!"

He thought on this new proposal of hers for a moment. "I do trust Cummings completely. He's quick witted and resourceful. Perhaps, acting in tandem, they could succeed in searching the Frenchmen's living quarters."

"When?" she asked.

"That depends on the Frenchmen's schedule. The search would need to be conducted when they're away. The difficulty will also be to determine when the servants are away. I'll put Cummings on that."

"I'm feeling hopeful."

He wished he did. He could not feel that anything they were doing could result in Hutch's safe return. They were merely eliminating theories of his whereabouts.

"May I ask a favor?" She looked up at him, much like an exuberant child.

"Of course."

"No matter what time it is, please come to me after you leave Brook's tonight. I shan't be able to sleep until I know what's occurred."

He sighed. Why was it he had so difficult a time refusing this woman's requests? "Very well."

THAT NIGHT, IN his fine, crested equipage, he met Messieurs Allard and Clavette outside their lodgings. The Frenchmen must be without fortune. They had not undertaken the expense of joining London's most distinguished men's clubs but relied instead on being guests of those men who had paid the hefty membership fees.

Monty was skeptical of why these foreigners would be so obsessed with befriending Englishmen who served at the highest levels of government. Unless they had been sent here for that purpose. At Brook's, he introduced the Frenchmen to the leading Whigs who gathered there.

"I believe my new friends," Monty said, indicating the Frenchmen, "were first seduced by the ruling party as they mingled at White's."

"Oh, no, no!" Monsieur Allard protested. "We merely wish to understand the workings of your British government, and the best way to do so, we have found, is to become acquainted with those who are most prominently involved. Already, reading the London newspapers has become so much more interesting now that we personally know some of these men in positions of power."

"It's most generous of you," Monsieur Clavette said to Monty, "to include us in your entertainments."

The men played Faro for modest stakes and partook of a late supper. While eating, Monty asked the more talkative of the two, "How long have you been an exile?"

Monsieur Allard's face took on a forlorn look. "It pains me to admit I've spent more time out of the country of my birth than I did in it. My father was able to save much of his fortune early on and relocate to Switzerland." His voice became guttural. "We despise Napoleon and everything he stood for."

Monsieur Clavette nodded in assent.

As convincing as the Frenchmen were, Monty knew that one here on a mission from the crazed former emperor would have been schooled to say those very things.

"It sounds as if you might be contemplating making England your permanent home."

"I cannot speak for my friend," Allard said, "but I am contemplating it. I always thought I'd return to France once that monster was no longer in power, but I'm waiting to see. There have been rumors in France that Boney may try to come back. I will never be subjugated to that fiend."

The Frenchman said all the right things. "I don't blame you, old fellow."

"I understand the Duke of Wellington will sit in the House of Lords next week," Allard said. "Meeting him would be the greatest honor."

A blatant hint. "I cannot say that I'm in the duke's inner circle, though we are acquainted. If you come to the gallery next week, perhaps I can introduce you."

The two Frenchmen exchanged gleeful glances, and Clavette answered. "That would be most generous of you."

It was only later that night—or morning, actually—that Monty regretted his offer. What if the duke were the target of the assassin? What if these men had been sent here to kill Wellington?

⁂

LUCY HAD AVOIDED dressing for bed. She was determined to stay awake until his lordship called. It had grown very cold, and before they had gone to bed, the servants had built fires in her bedchamber and in the library, where she was curled up on the sofa reading.

The library had been selected not only for its coziness on this frigid night but also because from this ground-floor chamber she would easily be able to hear his knock when Lord Montague called. She had no desire to force the servants to stay up late in order to admit his lordship into the house.

Because of the coolness, she had wrapped an ivory Kashmir shawl over the skimpy muslin gown she'd worn to dine alone.

At half past three, a humble knock sounded at the front door. She flung down her book and scurried into the entrance hall, coming to a stop just before the door. She'd instructed that the lanterns be left on all night, so she had only to swivel up the flap over the peep hole to be assured it was, indeed, Lord Montague calling at this hour.

"Thank you for coming," she greeted when opening the door to him.

"I feel beastly interfering with your sleep for this. There's not much to report."

Unconscious of what she was doing, she slipped her arm through his and guided him to the library where they sat upon the sofa near the fire. "I want to hear every single thing."

"They said nothing that could be construed as incriminating. In fact, Allard rather blatantly criticized Boney."

"Exactly what we should expect from a potential assassin working for Napoleon."

"My feelings exactly, though one thing did occur to me. . ."

She moved closer. "Do tell, my lord."

"The men were so eager to meet the Duke of Wellington, I wonder if he might be the target."

She gasped. "I can think of no one Bonaparte would rather see dead."

"There is that."

"Do you know the duke?"

Lord Montague shrugged. "Slightly. I foolishly said I might be able to introduce them when he sits in the House of Lords next week."

"If that is the case, we must endeavor to make certain the men are in no way armed."

"I will see to that."

"Have you spoken to your man about searching the Frenchmen's or the count's lodgings?"

"I have. In fact, he was planning to scout the situation this evening. Perhaps by tomorrow he will have a plan for him and your Hannah to conduct their own investigation."

"Hannah's to be left in the dark regarding the nature of the... shall we call it an *operation*? She still has not been told that Mr. Hutchinson is missing as it seemed unwise to have the news spread all over town. By the way, did your man show any kind of pleasure that he'd be seeing Hannah again?"

"How would I know? Men take no notice of such things." He straightened, and she knew he was about to leave.

"You're going to leave me, aren't you?" she asked, her voice conveying her need for companionship.

"I've inconvenienced you enough. You need sleep."

"And I've looked forward all night to your coming. You cannot imagine how intolerable it is being all alone in a vibrant city, especially for one like me, who's typically surrounded by most or all of my five siblings."

He turned to her, took both her hands in his, and spoke in a gentle voice. "I'm so sorry, Lucy."

It felt as if her heart had leapt from her chest. He'd called her by her first name. Not even her betrothed had ever spoken so intimately to her.

Chapter Fifteen

What the devil was he doing? Here he was, still clasping the hand of a woman who belonged to another. And not just any other. This was Hutch's betrothed. Monty had even taken the liberty of addressing Hutch's fiancée by her Christian name!

This woman had unknowingly saturated every pore of his existence. Even when they weren't together, she dominated his thoughts. In truth, he had taken to thinking of her as Lucy long before now. Not Hutch's Lucy. Just Lucy. The woman with whom *he* shared so much.

Moments ago, when she'd not wanted him to leave, it was as if she were voicing his own thoughts. He had not wanted to return to his lonely house, either. If only he could stay here. With her.

But he could not.

He was a man of honor. He could never betray Hutch. Even if Hutch did not love her, did not cherish her as Monty would, Lucy could be the instrument of saving Hutch's life. And right now, the most important thing in Monty's life was saving Hutch's.

He withdrew his hand and stood. It was best if he acted as if he had not just committed the unpardonable act of calling her by her Christian name.

"It grieves me to leave you. I, too, hail from a large family and don't relish going home to an empty house, but we do need to sleep. We need to have clear minds for what tomorrow brings. I'll return in the afternoon. Perhaps then we can devise a new plan of action." He had to leave now before he did something he would regret.

She looked even smaller as she sat there looking up at him, a dollop of white smothered by the sofa's red velvet. He fought the desire to draw her into his arms.

If he stayed another moment in her presence, he would do something that could destroy his self-respect. "Good night, Miss Beresford."

>>><<<

HAD LORD MONTAGUE slapped her across the face, she could not have felt more mortified. Moments earlier, hearing her name tumble so sweetly off his lips as his hands closed over hers had elevated her spirits more than a dozen glasses of champagne. But now she realized how deeply he regretted that slip of his tongue, that tender touch.

She was perplexed. How could he feel so close to her one moment and flee from her the next? Was that how rakes routinely acted with women who sparked nothing more than a casual interest?

In spite of the hour, she continued to sit there staring at the fire, incapable of thinking clearly. She could not go to her impersonal bedchamber. It was here in the library where she felt his presence. She could still hear the timbre of his manly voice, feel the pressure of his hands on hers, absorb the heat of him as if he still sat next to her.

She tried to recall the sound of Mr. Hutchinson's voice, but she could not. Yet he was the man she was supposed to spend the rest of her life with. He was the man her father had personally chosen. If anything had happened to him, she would be devastated. Finding him—and finding him unharmed—was paramount to her happiness.

Why, then, had Lord Montague become even more important to her? A day without seeing him was unimaginable.

But the way he'd so abruptly risen after their unexpected intimacy—she feared he must now be repulsed over his careless actions. In that moment of deflation, she feared she'd never see him again.

Then she was lifted from a dark abyss when she recalled he'd said he would see her tomorrow. With thoughts of what might transpire the following day, she finally drifted off to sleep on the library's sofa.

<hr />

"Your lordship might be interested to know that I took the liberty last evening to do reconnaissance at the Piccadilly lodgings of Misters Allard and Clavette, as well as at the mansion being leased by your Count von Gustafsen," Cummings said, and he lathered up his master's face for the morning shave.

"And what have you learned?"

"I suspect that the Frenchmen's pockets are not very deep. They have but a lone woman who comes midday to tidy their chambers and prepare a modest respite and pot of tea."

"What of a valet?"

Cummings shrugged. "Apparently, they do not use the services of such a person. I suppose it's possible their men may have stayed behind on the Continent. Passages on packet boats can cost dearly, I'm told."

Monty watched in the mirror as Cummings shaved him. "That might be the case. Did you have the opportunity to see what kind of locks are on the men's flat?"

"I did, my lord. It should be no difficulty whatsoever to secure entry."

No difficulty for Cummings, who had honed a variety of useful talents. "So you've decided to conduct the search?"

"With your lordship's permission—and the comely Miss Hannah assisting."

Now that Lucy had brought up the subject of an attraction between his valet and her lady's maid, Monty was giving it his due consideration. He supposed Cummings might very well be looking forward to the association with Lucy's so-called Hardheaded Hannah. "Of course, you have my permission. It's my understanding the Frenchmen are rarely home during the evenings. Should you like to start tonight?"

"Indeed, my lord." He swiped the razor's blade on a cloth and signaled his completion.

Monty stood. "I will have Miss Beresford alert her maid."

He had no expectations that anything suspicious would be found there, but he must be thorough. Now all that remained was to contrive a way for him and Lucy to be able to search the count's premises.

>>><<<

"I HAVE JUST received a note from Lord Montague," Lucy told Hannah as her maid was helping her into a freshly pressed lavender dress. "His lordship has undertaken a commission for the government. There is a possibility that men of our acquaintance—foreigners—might be working against the Crown, and his lordship needs to have their premises searched. His valet will be doing this. Tonight. And I've offered you to assist him. If you're agreeable."

Lucy was disappointed that his lordship had sent a note instead of coming in person, but she was hiding it well. Had he no intention of fulfilling his promise to call on her today?

Through her looking glass, Lucy watched Hannah for a reaction and was pleased to see the maid's face brighten.

"With Mr. Cummings?"

Lucy nodded.

"This very night?"

"Indeed."

"I know just what I'll wear! I've been saving that butter yellow dress you gave me for just such an occasion."

"Perhaps another time. I believe Mr. Cummings requested that you wear black. Remember, this is to be a clandestine search."

"So the foreigners are Scotsmen?"

Lucy's brows lowered. "No. They're French. Why did you think they were from Scotland?"

"You said they was from a clan."

"I said no such thing." Lucy searched her memory for what she'd said, then she remembered. "I said clandestine. That means secret."

Hannah glared. "Why did you not just say secret?"

"In the future, I shall endeavor to refrain from using big words." As she left her chamber, Lucy heard Lord Montague's voice. He had come!

She raced down the stairs to greet him.

"Good," he said. "I see you're dressed to pay morning calls."

Her head cocked, and she eyed him suspiciously. "Morning calls?"

"Yes. My sister awaits in the carriage. I have learned that this is the day Count von Gustafsen receives visitors. You and she are going to visit him today, while I will endeavor to search his house."

"You plan to search his home in daylight while he's there?" She looked incredulous.

"I do."

"And you worry about me putting myself in danger! That is a terrible idea."

He gave her a sly smile. "You must trust me on this."

After donning a pelisse which matched her dress and tying on a bonnet, she joined Lady Carrington in his lordship's coach.

"As delightful as it is to see you again, my dear Miss Beresford," Lady Carrington said, "I feel ridiculous paying a call on that Swedish count. It's not as if I'm acquainted with the man." She faced her brother. "And, I declare, Arthur, what is this fascination you've acquired over foreigners? One would think you're bereft of friends—

perfectly acceptable English friends—the way you're so devilishly eager to court these *un*-English men! And speaking of friends, where is your Mr. Hutchinson? I declare, you spend more time with his affianced than he does. What does he have to say about that?"

"I am merely keeping the lady company while my friend must be out of town."

Lucy recalled that Lady Carrington was reputed to be a gossip, so a slight prevarication was in order. "Your brother is keeping me company at Mr. Hutchinson's request, seeing as my cousin, Lord Devere, is away also."

"I suppose that's very good of you, Arthur. Goodness knows, Miss Beresford is far more respectable company than that friend of yours. Why you don't settle down and marry is beyond my feeble comprehension. It's a very good thing Mama and Papa are not here to see the scandalous reports of you in the newspapers."

"Pray, don't say it's a good thing our parents are no longer here."

"Of course you know I didn't mean it that way. Nary a day goes by I don't lament their loss." Lady Carrington faced Lucy once more. "It seemed rather like the count took a fancy to you when I introduced you to him the other night."

"He did not, at that time, know that Miss Beresford is betrothed to my friend. That has been rectified."

At the count's house, the threesome was shown to the upstairs drawing room, then the butler went to apprise the count of his callers. No one else shared the chamber. Lord Montague did not sit when the ladies did. He eyed Lucy. "I will find the necessary room.

⸻※⸻

AFTER MOVING TO the drawing room door, Monty paused and looked in every direction to assure himself no one was watching him. Then, he walked softly and descended the stairs like a cat on soft paws. He had purposely not asked the butler for directions. Since the necessary room was not his destination, his wandering of the house could be better explained by saying he was searching for the butler to ask directions if he were unfortunate enough to be discovered.

If one were to be keeping a prisoner at his London lodgings, Monty reasoned, the basement was the most logical place. Especially if the basement featured a wine cellar. Since the count did not entertain at night, it wasn't likely his servants would have a reason to use the cellar.

In the basement, he tiptoed past the kitchen, surprised to see no evidence of a cook or scullery maid. He supposed the count must rarely eat at home. And since the count had made no secret that he was not wealthy, it made sense for him to economize with a reduction of servants.

When Monty saw a lone woman standing in the scullery with her back to him, he ducked back. He waited several minutes until he heard her steps moving back to the kitchen through the connecting door.

As quietly as possible, Monty proceeded, passing the larder next. Few stores of food were in evidence. At the end of the narrow corridor was an arched timber door with a padlock. *Ah, this must be the wine cellar!*

Though it was locked, he suspected the count was not likely to be carrying around large household keys. Which meant it might just be possible that the key could be stowed somewhere near here. Monty looked around. His hope that it might be hanging from a hook on the wall was soon dashed. Next, he went back to the larder and began to open drawers. In the third one, he located a key.

It easily slid into the lock. Praying he'd find a bound-and-gagged Hutch there, he swung open the door. His heart drummed as he peered into the dark chamber. What a pity he had no candle. He stepped onto the cellar's dirt floor and walked into the darkness. There was nothing near the door. He could tell the chamber was fairly deep.

Possibly thirty feet. Perhaps the wine was further in where it would be cooler. Hopefully, Hutch, too. As he strode into its depths, the door slammed closed.

His blood chilled at the sound of the lock clicking into place.

Chapter Sixteen

The count must not be accustomed to receiving callers, Lucy thought, as they waited a considerable period of time for him. Was he needing to be both shaved and dressed? She wondered if he'd brought his valet with him from Sweden.

Though the address of the house he was letting was prestigious, the house itself had certainly seen its better days. The furnishings were of another era—perhaps as far back as the Tudor period. The upholstery was so faded, she passed the time trying to guess what color it had been originally. If she were one to wager, her money would have been on the notion that the thinning, grayish brocade may once have been a vivid green.

While she mused, she had also been forced to hear the seemingly never-ending saga of Lady Carrington's busy morning that enumerated a pot of tepid chocolate she demanded to be reheated, a swollen head from a poor night's sleep, her maid bringing her the wrong dress, and complaints about the tardiness of the wetnurse who was attending the lady's infant son.

With unexpected pleasure, Lucy greeted the count when he finally entered the chamber.

"How honored I am to have two such lovely ladies calling at my humble abode," he said as he made a display of bending his lanky frame to kiss each of their hands.

He sat on a high-backed, throne-like chair opposite the sofa where they sat.

"How long have you resided in this house?" Lady Carrington asked.

"I have been here since I came to London two months ago."

"I remember when I was still a girl I accompanied my mother to see the Duchess of York in a house very near here," Lady Carrington said.

"I am honored to have made the acquaintance of that lady's husband."

The Regent's eldest brother, the Duke of York. "How fortune you were, my lady, to have grown up in the Capital," Lucy said.

"Indeed, my lady," the count concurred, "as patriotic as I am toward my own homeland, I cannot say growing up in Sweden was especially enjoyable. Our winters are so dark and bleak."

Lady Carrington launched into a long story about one winter she spent in Scotland and recounted her own experiences with days that looked like nights.

As the conversation dragged on about a variety of banal topics, Lucy's attention waned, and her worry mounted. What was Lord Montague doing? He'd had ample time to make a cursory inspection of every chamber in the house. The house was not large.

What if he'd been caught? What if he were in danger?

She was actually surprised his sister had not yet blurted out a query regarding her brother's whereabouts. The only explanation Lucy could think of for the woman's silence on the subject (a rarity indeed) must be that she suspected her brother—who had told her nothing of their true purpose here—must be having digestive difficulties, and she probably deemed it too delicate a subject to broach in public.

For that, Lucy was thankful. It wouldn't do for the count—especially if he were the assassin—to know that Lord Montague was snooping about his house. Her stomach clenched. What if the count had found his lordship searching where he wasn't supposed to be? Was that why the count had taken so long to join them in the drawing room.

⇢⇢⇢⇠⇠⇠

WHO IN THE devil had locked him in? Was it the count? Was he the assassin? Did he mean to kill Monty? Monty wondered why he hadn't heard anyone.

His first action was to search the cellar for Hutch. It was impossible to see anything in the total darkness. He bumped into a barrel as he moved through the darkness. Good lord, was Hutch's body stuffed into it? He could scarcely breathe as his trembling body bent to sniff at it. Thank God. It was wine.

He moved further in, hoping he would find Hutch merely with his hands and feet bound and a cloth tied around his mouth. But he found nothing. A double disappointment: now his own life was soon to be as questionable as his friend's.

His attention then turned to the daunting task of getting out of this locked chamber before something unthinkable happened to him. Unfortunately, the only way in or out of the cellar was through that locked door. And there was no way to open it from the inside.

Or was there? He felt all around the door and in the process snagged a splinter in his index finger. Before he could even wince, he found something to give him hope. The hinges were on the inside!

Disappointingly, they had likely been there untouched for at least two centuries. Adding to that disappointment, he had no tools or instruments to help dislodge them. All he had was his own strength and whatever ingenuity he could muster. He tried lifting the pin from the bottom hinge first, but it would not budge. He then removed his boot and banged at it from the bottom, but in the complete darkness, it was difficult to tell if it moved.

His next effort to lift from the top hinge was not successful, and he returned his attention to the bottom one. His fingernail detected a hairline gap that hadn't been there during his first try, but his nail was too thick to breach the gap. He ripped a brass button from his jacket, and with the sturdy thread from it, he wedged it into the gap, circling the pin. To his relief, the pin moved! He was then able to pull it out.

The process was repeated for the top hinge, and moments later, he removed the door from its hinges.

It must have made a noise, for the cook raced into the corridor. When she saw him standing there attempting to restore the door, her mouth gaped open. "Did I lock you in there, sir?" Clearly his clothing had identified him as a man of wealth and breeding.

Thank God his jailer wasn't the count! "Indeed, madam. I was in search of the necessary room."

"I am terribly sorry, sir. I thought I must have forgotten to lock the cellar. You should have called out. Anyway, you'll find the necessary room on the ground floor just behind the porter's room, which is next to the front door."

"Thank you."

Moments later, Monty returned to the drawing room. The count stood to greet him, a puzzled look on his face while the relief on Lucy's face was palpable.

"There you are!" Lady Carrington said. Then, she addressed their host. "My brother must have gotten lost looking for the necessary room."

Eyeing Monty, the count's brows elevated. "It's a pleasure to have you, my lord."

"What a pity that I won't be able to stay longer." Monty's gaze flicked from the count to his sister and back. "I'm sure my sister has taken enough of your valuable time."

"Your sister's delightful."

"Nevertheless, she is a most determined talker." Monty winked at her.

"You sound just like Carrington," she chided.

Lucy stood, and his sister took her cue.

Once they were in the Montague coach, his sister wished to have her curiosity assuaged. "Are you unwell, Arthur?"

"I'm fine now, but I believe I'll go home."

After they dropped off his sister, Lucy wanted a complete report. "I take it you did not find Mr. Hutchinson?"

"Sadly, I did not."

"I was dreadfully worried about you. You must tell me everything."

He was oddly pleased that she had worried about him. "I believed if Hutchinson were being held there, the count's wine cellar would be the logical place." He explained what happened to him while she gasped and clutched at her heaving bosom. "Though there was a period of time there where I was convinced the count was keeping me prisoner and I would join Hutch in his fate, I think the count has now been exonerated."

"I will own, it is less likely, but I'm not ready yet to discount anyone."

"Perhaps my valet will learn more tonight at the Frenchmen's lodgings."

A frown wrinkled her brow. "You're sure Hannah will be safe?"

"I would trust Cummings with my own sisters' lives."

"Will you come to me late tonight—after Mr. Cummings reports to you?"

He did not respond for a moment. His thoughts went to the previous night and his unpardonable actions. He was afraid he would go even further if he found himself alone with her again tonight. Because of his friendship with Hutch, he could not allow himself to come to her tonight. There was something incredibly alluring about Miss Lucy Beresford and her effect upon him.

"I believe your Hannah may be able to give you a report. Of course, if they find your betrothed . . . I will make sure you two are reunited."

For hours later, he was unable to dispel from his memory the forlorn look on Lucy's face.

"How do I look?" Hannah asked her mistress that night as she twirled around Miss Beresford's bedchamber, her gaze riveted to the looking glass that reflected a lovely mourning dress her mistress had passed down to her. Hannah was not accustomed to wearing such fine clothing, but it was important to her that she look her best for the handsome Mr. Cummings tonight.

"You look lovely. You'll sweep Mr. Cummings off his feet."

The two ladies then descended the stairs. Hannah's partner for the evening was to collect her at ten o'clock. To her surprise, he was already waiting. Fifteen minutes early! She felt as if she were a princess as Mr. Cummings offered his arm and led her to his master's fine coach.

The carriage ride took only a couple of moments, but Mr. Cummings had told the coachman to stop several houses away from the one they were scheduled to search.

"If the outside door of the flats is locked," he said, "I will retreat to where I cannot be seen, and you will then knock upon the door and convey to the landlady that you're looking for respectable lodgings. Tell her you're a seamstress at a fine shop on Conduit Street and try to make conversation with her for as long as possible. During that time, I will endeavor to sneak into the premises." He held up a ring holding a variety of keys.

"You can count on me." She would not let him down, even if she had to launch into praise of every item in the landlady's chambers. She stayed in the coach, gawking through the window as he strode to the building where the suspected Scotsmen resided. Then she remembered they weren't Scotsmen. They were some kind of foreigners who meant harm to her country.

Which made her a heroine. And Mr. Cummings a hero. What a fine man he was!

He tried the outer door, but it must have been locked for he retreated and came to stand behind the carriage, nodding silently at her as he passed by.

She knew what to do.

A moment after she knocked upon the door, a woman's voice said, "What do you want?" without attempting to open the door.

"Forgive me, madam, for the lateness of the hour, but I've had to work late at Mrs. Moreland's shop on Conduit, and this is the first opportunity I've had to come here to make inquiries. I've heard very nice things about your place and was hoping I could see about securing lodgings here. Dare I ask if you could admit me?" Hannah knew every woman in London would have heard about Mrs. Moreland's fine shop.

Seconds later, the door swung open, and Hannah was facing a silver-haired woman who had thrown a wrapper around her. "Good evening. I'm Mrs. Broadbent. As it happens, I do have chambers for a refined female available on this very floor. Men reside on the upper floors. Should you like me to show you the chambers?"

Hannah took the liberty of gently closing the door behind her, hoping the woman wouldn't go back and lock it. "Indeed I would."

The two of them strolled down the side corridor which ran along the narrow, wooden staircase. It led to a pair of chambers that consisted of a front parlor and an adjacent bedchamber. In the parlor, a woolen rug covered much of the wooden floor. The chamber featured one upholstered armchair in front of the fire and a small table with two wooden chairs.

"I must commend you, Mrs. Broadbum, on the cleanliness of the place," Hannah said. "So tidy!"

"It's Broad*bent*. When one wishes to appeal to the best sort of people, one must make every effort to project the proper image. Many of our residents engage the services of Mrs. Williams, who tidies their chambers."

"How very convenient." Hannah took her time moving to a little buffet where tea things were stored and stood there for several seconds before striding toward the fireplace where a small scuttle of coal was kept. "This looks a most comforting place to live—especially on a cold winter's night."

Next, a smiling Mrs. Broadbent strolled into the modest bedchamber. A single, uncovered rope bed hugged one wall. A bedside table was topped with a candlestick. Pegs hung from the walls and a waist-high linen press was on the wall opposite the bed. A single wooden chair beside the fireplace was the room's only other furnishing.

"Ah," Hannah said, "another comfortable-looking chamber. I've got just the counterpane to fit this bed."

"Mind you," Mrs. Broadbent said, "this is my most modest chamber. I've found that the single women who come here are those who must toil at respectable occupations, whereas the gentlemen that reside above are men of means, and their chambers are much fancier."

"Then you're saying the men who live here are most respectable? Because that is very important to me." Hannah knew she had to keep talking to give Mr. Cummings time to conduct his search.

"Oh, yes, miss! In fact, we have at present two gentlemen—French they are—who have connections to the slain French Royal Family. Very proper they are. You won't believe how finely they dress."

It must be them Frenchies who were submerging our government. Was submerging the right word? Miss Beresford would know. Hannah didn't see how Mrs. Broadsomething could be civil to those horrid men. Hannah never had no use for French people. But, alas, she must pretend otherwise. She had to keep the landlady talking. "That's good to know—not that I'm likely to cross paths with the fine gentlemen."

"I suppose, if you are employed by Mrs. Moreland, you know all about dressing beautifully."

Hannah preened as the landlady's admiring gaze whisked over the fine mourning dress she wore. "Indeed I do. And I understand about your Frenchmen dressing well. It does seem to come naturally to the French. That's why Mrs. Moreland is such a sought-after modiste. She's French, you know." That was something Hannah had learned from Miss Beresford's cousins, who patronized her.

"Oh, I did not."

"Born and bred in France, but she married an Englishman. That's why her name don't sound French."

Hannah made a production of looking carefully about the chamber. "You understand I work long hours. But my pay is very good."

"I expect you'll be wanting to know how much it will cost you to live here?"

Hannah swallowed. "Indeed."

"For a nice lady like you, I can let it go for a half a guinea a month." Mrs. Broadbent's eyes rolled upward. "The Frenchmen pay half a guinea a week, but in addition to being much finer, their chambers are larger. They've got two bedchambers with a parlor between them."

"I think a half a guinea a month sounds very reasonable for such a respectable address. It would be so nice to live in a fine neighborhood near the fine ladies I'm accustomed to working with." Hannah moved to the fireplace where the scuttle was empty, then crossed the chamber to open the linen press. It was empty.

"And this should be walking distance to your place of employment."

"Tomorrow, I shall endeavor to see just how far it is for me to walk from Mrs. Moreland's to your lodgings, Mrs. Broadbutt." She wondered if Mr. Cummings had finished his search yet. She couldn't stay here much longer. She'd already run out of things to comment upon.

"Broad*bent's* the name."

"Dear me, I'm hopeless with names—and fancy words." Hannah strolled back into the parlor and circled it once more, deliberately stopping to gaze at each item in the chamber. She could see that the landlady, whatever her silly name was, was moving for the outer door. It was still too soon. She must distract her.

"Cats! I would have to bring my cat. He's very well behaved. Please say you will allow me to bring my little Snuggles."

The woman's brows lowered. "Is he loud?"

Hannah effected an outraged expression. "I will have you know my Snuggles is the best, most quiet little furball you ever saw. I know you will love my Snuggles, Mrs. Broadbottom."

The woman's eyes narrowed to slits and she did not sound amused. "Not Broad*bottom*. Broad*bent*."

Hannah was powerless not to steal a glance at the woman's backside. If her opinion were solicited, she would say Mrs. Broadwhatever was, indeed, possessed of a broad bottom.

Keep talking. "Do forgive me. As I told you, I'm hopeless with names. It is a good thing I'm good with a needle. And you must allow that cats are far better inside pets than dogs are. Do you not agree, Mrs. Broad . . ."

"*Bent.* I suppose cats are quieter than dogs, but I always favored dogs meself."

"You would change yer mind if you saw the home where Lady Harriett Beresford lives over on Curzon Street. She has no less than three cats, and they are permitted free rein of the entire house. They're quite adorable. Of course, not as adorable as my Snuggles." Hannah was almost beginning to believe she possessed a cat named Snuggles.

The landlady sighed. "I suppose it will be acceptable for you to bring your Snuggles."

How long would it take Mr. Cummings to search the Frenchies' rooms? Surely he was done now. "How did you know my kitty's name?" *Keep stalling.*

"You told me."

Hannah thwacked her forehead. "So I did!" She held out her hand that was gloved in black. "Yes, Mrs. Broadbender, I think this will do very well. By the way, I am Miss Cummings." She really wished she were one Mrs. Cummings.

After the landlady clasped her hand, Hannah asked, "Will it be permissible for me to finalize this tomorrow?"

"Oh, yes, indeed."

Hannah prayed Mr. Cummings was finished. "I will return then. Thank you so much for allowing me to intruse upon your evening." Was *intruse* the correct word? Why was she acting like Miss Beresford and using them fancy words? Why could she not have just apologized for coming so late?

"It was my pleasure to make your acquaintance, Miss Cummings. You are just the sort of respectable tradeswoman I would enjoy having as a resident here. And it's been a long while since I've had the companionship of another woman."

"You make me feel so welcome."

As the women moved from the chambers, Hannah was relieved to see no signs of Mr. Cummings. She only hoped he awaited her in the carriage. She was careful to reach the door first and clasp the handle to cover up the fact it had not been relocked. "Again, thank you so much."

Back in the carriage, she faced Lord Montague's fine-looking valet. "Well?" she asked.

"You did very well. I was able to enter the building moments after you. I stealthily crept upstairs to the Frenchmen's chambers, managed to open the lock, and conducted my search. Unfortunately, I found nothing that could in any way be construed as suspicious."

"Then we're not going to be heroes?"

Mr. Cummings gave a shy smile. "I suppose not."

"I hope yer Lord Montague allows us to help him some more."

"That is a hope I wholeheartedly share, Miss . . . Hannah. Could you reveal to me your surname?"

Surname? "Does that mean my last name?"

"Indeed, it does."

"Then I'm Miss Hannah Makepiece."

"It has been an honor to partner with you, Miss Makepiece."

She felt like a grand lady.

CHAPTER SEVENTEEN

Lucy stayed up late, anxious to learn what Hannah and Lord Montague's valet had discovered. To pass the time, she went to Harriet's menagerie and played with her cousin's pets. She was thankful Harriett's pet mouse had crossed over to Pet Heaven, though. Lucy had always been embarrassed to admit how terrified she was over the miniscule mouse. Harriett's cats, on the other hand, delighted Lucy, especially the little orange one named Pumpkin. He'd recently started climbing into bed with Lucy each night.

When Hannah finally came, Lucy was disappointed to learn their trip had turned up no new information, but it was difficult to be too sad when Hannah was bursting with excitement.

Even after Lucy went to bed—with Pumpkin softly purring beside her—she kept thinking about her maid's exuberance. An outing like Hannah had experienced that night was rarely available to one who'd spent her life in servitude. How lucky Lucy was to have been born to such privilege. She vowed to see to it that Hannah got more opportunities to shed her duties and enjoy herself—hopefully with a man she felt as fondly toward as she did her Mr. Cummings.

Lucy did grow morose the next day after Hannah, still ecstatic over her outing with Mr. Cummings, finished dressing her hair. She had selected a becoming pale yellow dress but had no expectations of seeing Lord Montague that day. He had made it clear the previous day that he saw no reason to be in her pocket at her whim. Which was completely understandable. He must be accustomed to being in the presence of beautiful women whose knowledge of the world substantially exceeded hers.

If only one of her cousins would come home. What good did wearing a lovely dress do when there was no one to see her and no place to go?

As she sat in the library penning letters to her sisters back home at Tilford Hall, the footman informed her that Lord Montague was calling. Her heart leapt. "Please show him to this chamber."

Today, with the velvet draperies drawn to flood the chamber with sunshine and with no fire warming the room, it wasn't as intimate as it had been the last time the two of them had sat together in this very room. Her pulse quickened at the memory. He'd held her hands. He'd called her *Lucy*. Then, to her sorrow, he'd regretted his actions and fled.

From behind the desk, she watched the door. Soon, his lordship filled that doorway, and she was powerless not to stare as he just stood there regarding her in much the same way as she regarded him. His broad shoulders filled out his coat. Her gaze swept over his long, rangy legs that terminated into a pair of black boots as shiny as glass.

Apparently, his lordship did not intend to enter the library. Was he avoiding it because of what had happened here two nights ago?

"Good day, my lord."

A slow smile brought an immediate softening of his features. "Good day to you, Miss Beresford. I've come in my phaeton. I intend for us to take a long, leisurely ride through the park. Even if it's not the fashionable hour. We can discuss where our inquiries should go from here."

She felt as if she were soaring in one of those balloons over Hyde Park. He'd come! And he was permitting her to be a full partner in his inquiries and didn't abhor her companionship! "I'll just fetch my bonnet."

"Don't let the bright sun fool you. It's beastly cold outside. You'll need a pelisse or shawl or something warm today."

Wearing a bonnet and a pelisse that matched her dress, she sat beside him on the phaeton's perch. It was shrewd of him to select an open conveyance. Now there would be neither a need nor room for a chaperone. They could be alone together in a perfectly respectable way.

"Even though I was disappointed we didn't find Hutch at the Swede's or the Frenchmen's," he began, "we have likely eliminated two things. Our mutual friend has probably not committed suicide, and he's probably not being held in London." He pulled back on the reins and turned to her. "I still have hope your fiancé's being held somewhere. I just wish I knew where."

"As do I."

"There's one thing that keeps bothering me," he began.

"Me, too. Why do you think someone forged Mr. Hutchinson's letter to get his female friend out of London?"

His lordship's mouth dropped open. "That's the very thing that's been plaguing me. Pray, Miss Beresford, are you reading my thoughts?"

She favored him with a smile. "Not that. It's just that we've been together so much, I suspect we're beginning to see things with a single vision."

The features on his face softened as he regarded her. "Back to your question, I cannot conceive any plausible explanation for it."

"Nor can I."

They entered the gates of Hyde Park. Even though it wasn't late enough in the afternoon to be the fashionable hour, nor was it a warm day, the day's radiant sunshine still brought out a goodly number of strollers and open conveyances. His lordship nodded at several people, both male and female, but he didn't stop to talk to any of them.

"What do you think we should do next?"

She shrugged. "I suppose we need to wait until the Frenchmen come to the House of Lords. If they're armed, that should tell us what we need to know." *That they planned to murder the Duke of Wellington.*

"I will discuss that possibility with Lord Stewart. I mean to request he have a number of men there to thwart any assassination attempt."

"It is a pity we can't avert something like that *before* the event, but the only way to prove guilt is to catch one in the act."

"True."

Another phaeton pulled up beside them. "Good day, my lord. Miss Beresford," the count greeted, doffing his shiny black hat. "I see your lordship is taking good care of his friend's betrothed." A hint of bitterness in his voice indicated a lack of sincerity.

Lord Montague brought his horse to a stop and faced the Swede. "There is nothing I wouldn't do for my friend, not that it's any great hardship to escort the delightful Miss Beresford around town."

"Perhaps the two of you will accompany me to Vauxhall Gardens sometime soon. I've heard much about it but have never had the pleasure of experiencing its offerings."

"Perhaps we can," Lord Montague said. He then touched his hat and continued on. The count turned off onto an intersecting path.

Lucy was unable to dispel the feeling that the count insinuated Lord Montague was attempting to displace Mr. Hutchinson in her affections. Did the man not know what an unequal alliance that would be?

Or . . . had the count the perceptiveness to realize how attracted she had become to the earl? From the first moment she'd realized how profoundly Lord Montague affected her, she'd tried to fight it. She was promised to another, to his lordship's closest friend, to the man selected by her worshipped father. She would never terminate the betrothal—that would have to be done by Mr. Hutchinson. Since the day she'd arrived in the Capital, she had planned to allow him to be released from the obligation, if that was what he wanted.

She suspected it was.

Of course, that could mean she'd soon be free again. Could it be the count was jealous because he had his eye on Lucy's fortune? After all, her papa had set aside very handsome dowries for each of his daughters. It wouldn't have taken much effort to learn of those arrangements. It was more surprising that he hadn't learned of Mr. Hutchinson's offer for her.

Lord Montague's dark brows lowered. "I believe we were followed here," he said, drawing Lucy out of her reverie.

"By whom?"

"Count von Gustafsen."

"Just to ask us to accompany him to Vauxhall?"

He shrugged. "Perhaps. Perhaps not."

A thought occurred to her that stole away her breath. "Do you suppose he learned about your being in his wine cellar?"

"His cook certainly could have told him." He drew a deep breath. "Give me your word you will never see that man alone."

"I have given you my word already. I'm to send for you if he even calls."

"That's right."

"It was far too bold of us to go to his house in daylight while servants were about. It would have been better to conduct a search at night when everyone was asleep."

"It's too late now. That's the problem with novices like us. And Hutch. I just hope to God Hutch's naiveté hasn't cost him his life."

Without thinking of what she was doing, she gripped his arm. Her insides plunged. She had not really considered that her fiancé would be dead. She had discussed it as a possibility, but it had all been so abstract. She'd not actually believed it. Until now. Suddenly she was possessed with an unshakable feeling that he was not alive.

A tear trailed down her cheek.

Lord Montague slowed, eyeing her. Then he flicked the ribbons and urged on his horse, but instead of following the main path, he turned onto a little-used lane that led to a thick copse of trees and underbrush and pulled to a stop. They were completely alone.

He faced her, those dark eyes of his searching her sorrowful face with concern. Then he drew her into his embrace, his powerful arms closing tightly around her.

It was the most comforting gesture she had ever experienced. Yet she burst into tears that shook her body. All the while he held her and murmured her name. *Lucy.*

She wept and wept, and his hold on her never relinquished. When her tears finally waned, she became embarrassed. She hated to face him with swollen eyes and red nose. Even worse, she feared she had ruined his fine coat with a mixture of tears and the French rouge she wore every day. She whimpered and sucked in a long breath. "Forgive me for being such a ninny."

He spoke with uncharacteristic gentleness. "You're not a ninny. You fear Hutchinson's dead, do you not?"

She nodded somberly.

"I hate to bring you such distress, but I share your fears." From his pocket, he withdrew a handkerchief and offered it to her.

She turned away, wiped her face, and blew her nose into it. "Thank you, my lord. I shall have my maid launder it."

He smiled and took up the ribbons. "We must return to the main path before I'm accused of ruining you. You know what my reputation is."

※※※

ON THE RETURN to Curzon Street, he did not speak. He was too muddled. Guilt coursed through him like heated brandy. He had no right to crave Hutch's fiancée, but he did. She'd invaded his waking hours as well as his dreams.

Seeing her cry had ignited emotions he'd been suppressing. He'd needed to feel her in his arms, to try to offer comfort. He'd needed her more than she had needed him.

What a disgusting rake he'd proven himself to be! When he'd drawn her into his arms, he'd not had a prurient thought in his head. But once he felt the delicacy of her, the slight swell of her bosom pressed against him, he'd grown painfully erect.

By God, he wanted this woman more than he'd ever wanted anything. And as long as Hutch drew breath—and he hoped that would be for the rest of his own life—he would be denied her.

Even though Monty had fallen desperately in love with her.

Chapter Eighteen

This was the day the Frenchmen—and the Duke of Wellington—were going to attend a session at the House of Lords. Lucy would love to be in that gallery today, but at present, women were prohibited. What a pity. When her mother was young, she had been among the ladies who were permitted to attend hearings in the trial of Warren Hastings in the House of Commons, but women had since been excluded.

That Lord Montague did not also exclude her from his inquiries boosted her already-favorable opinion of him. She had found him to be exceedingly fair-minded and had come to dismiss the accounts of him she'd read in the newspapers, the ones that painted him to be a rake who recklessly played with women's hearts.

"'Tis another sunny day," Hannah said, standing back to observe her mistress now that the morning's dressing ritual was complete. "That pink dress is most fetching on you."

"Then I fancy a nice walk. Where should we go?"

Hannah shrugged. "The park?"

Though Green Park was closest, Lucy preferred the vastness of Hyde Park and its many different terrains. In some parts of that park, she could imagine herself on a lovely country estate. "A very good suggestion. Let us go to Hyde Park."

Hyde Park had become even more alluring since that day she'd been there with Lord Montague. The day he'd drawn her into his arms. The very memory of it thinned her breath.

Since it was not yet noon, few people were enjoying the park. They entered at a pedestrian entrance off of Park Lane and began to stroll along a narrow path toward the Serpentine.

"You enjoyed yourself so much with Mr. Cummings the other night, I've decided you will have one night each week free of any duties. Obviously, it can't be when I will need you to help me prepare for, say, going to Almack's, but if I've no formal occasions, you will have your choice in when you'd like to take time for your own pleasure."

"That's very kind of you. If only Mr. Cummings wished to be with me, and if only his master would be as generous as you."

"I believe Lord Montague will be a most generous master." The truth was, Lucy could believe nothing negative about his lordship anymore. He'd earned her complete admiration.

His insistence on chaperones and riding in open carriages when possible indicated he was more concerned over her reputation than she was. When she had first become acquainted with him, she'd believed her virtue safe because she did not appeal to him. But now . . . as difficult as it was to believe, she thought perhaps he did not find her completely undesirable. That thought sent her heart fluttering in a most uncommon fashion. And she could not deny that she found him to be the most desirable man in all the kingdom.

They turned onto an even narrower lane that was shaded by trees which had recently come into full bloom after a harsh winter. This lonely stretch of park reminded her of where Lord Montague had taken her that day he'd held her so tenderly while she wept. Its memory intensified those vibrations that strummed through her. How she longed to be held by him. Be kissed by him. Be loved by him.

She suddenly became aware of a pounding of horses and whirled around to observe a coach-and-four speeding toward them. This lane was never intended to convey carriages. What was the driver thinking?

She and Hannah were forced to scurry from the path to avoid being knocked down by the swift-moving coach.

The coachman yanked on the reins for a sudden stop right where she and Hannah had been walking. The doors flung open, and four masked men rushed toward the females.

Her heart pounding prodigiously, Lucy grabbed Hannah's hand and raced into the undergrowth. Hannah's foot must have caught on a tree root for she plunged forward. Lucy stopped to help her up.

That was all it took to give their assailants time to catch up with them. Lucy managed a piercing scream. Cursing, two of the men grabbed her. She kicked one in the shins, and let out another cry for help, but one of her captors tied a filthy cloth over her mouth.

"That'll shut 'er up." The vulgar man then proceeded to bind her wrists and ankles with coarse rope. Tightly.

The two other men gagged and bound a screaming Hannah, then both women were tossed into the coach as if they were rolls of soiled carpet.

>>><<<

BEFORE HE HAD gone to the House of Lords, Monty had arranged to meet with Lord Stewart.

"Men, this is Lord Montague. I wanted you to be able to recognize him," Lord Stewart told the soldiers who had gathered in his Whitehall office. "He and two other men—Frenchmen—will enter the White Chamber where the Lords meet. It's those two men you are to watch. There's a possibility they may have come here to assassinate someone. We fear the Duke of Wellington may be the target. It goes without saying you are to guard the duke as well."

Six of the soldiers wore Guards uniforms. Another dozen men were out-of-uniform soldiers.

After the Whitehall meeting, Monty collected the Frenchmen at their lodgings. They wore no swords. He eyed the garments they wore. There was no way a weapon like a pistol or knife was kept in their snug-fitting breeches or their well-tailored coats. Nevertheless, he, too, would keep a close eye on them.

"It is so very kind of you to accord us this honor," Monsieur Allard said.

The three men entered the Palace of Westminster together, then Monty showed them the way to the gallery while he took his seat on a bench in the middle of the House of Lords chamber. He recognized, both in the gallery and on the floor of the house, the men who'd been at Lord Stewart's earlier.

No important legislation was to be voted upon today, so the items on the agenda were ticked off, one after another, in a speedy fashion. The Duke of Wellington, whom Stewart had warned about the potential threat, stayed until the end. When the gavel came down to terminate the day's activities, Monty approached the duke, nodding up to the gallery to indicate the Frenchmen could now be introduced to the Hero of Waterloo. This was the first time in several years that Monty had spoken to the duke. Now strands of silver threaded through his dark locks.

Despite the fact that Wellington was not a tall man, he was said by women to be most handsome. His eyes were on level with Monty's shoulders when they addressed one another. "It's good to have you back in the chamber," Monty said.

"It's gratifying to be back." The duke smiled. "I've been told you have Frenchmen with you who are desirous of meeting me."

"Indeed, Your Grace. Here they come."

The Frenchmen respectfully approached, and Monty said, "Your Grace, may I present to you Messieurs Allard and Clavette?"

The men shook hands.

"I cannot tell you how honored I am to meet the man who defeated that monster, Napoleon. My countrymen owe you a debt of gratitude we will never be able to repay."

"I appreciate that, especially since so many casualties were inflicted upon your countrymen in that recent battle."

"It is lamentable that blood must be shed to claim a satisfying victory," Monsieur Clavette said. It was the longest sentence Monty had ever heard him utter.

The chamber soon cleared out, and he restored the Frenchmen to their home. During the drive, they gushed their appreciation. Monty was thankful there had been no assassination attempt, but he felt a bit embarrassed that he'd prepared the Foreign Secretary for the threat for nothing. The unarmed Frenchmen had behaved impeccably and were genuinely humbled to be introduced to the Duke of Wellington. Which did seem to reinforce their stated disdain for Napoleon. Monty felt almost certain now that his suspicions about the Frenchmen had been wrong all along.

He supposed he needed to start all over. He'd put too much trust in Harmon's letter to his sweetheart, too much hope that they would find the assassin among the newcomers at Almack's. Had Harmon tossed out that reference to Almack's because he was not of the *ton* himself and all he had known about the *ton* was their exclusive affiliation with that bastion of Society located on King Street?

Monty found himself wondering how Hutch had gone about his investigation. He admired his friend for maintaining secrecy but wished he'd included one more person, namely himself, in the inquiries.

Lucy would be anxious to learn what had transpired in the House of Lords that day, so after he said farewell to the Frenchmen, he went straight to Curzon Street.

The youthful footman who answered her door did not readily admit Monty. "My mistress is not in."

Mindful of Lucy's lamentations about knowing no one and having little to do in London, he was puzzled. "Do you know where she's gone?" Monty asked.

"I heard her tell her maid who accompanied her that they were going to Hyde Park."

"How long ago did they leave?"

The footman's face collapsed. "It was still morning when they left."

Monty's gut plunged. It was nearly nightfall now. Something was wrong. "It was just the two women? On foot?"

"Yes, my lord."

Fear pulsed through him. She was in trouble.

He had to go to the park. But what good would that do so many hours after she'd left for there? The park was so massive, and now that it was dark, it would be impossible to search. Still, he had to try. There was nothing else he could do.

Chapter Nineteen

Those evil men had not blindfolded her or Hannah. If only they had. That they didn't must mean they didn't care if she saw where she was being taken. *They mean to kill us.* More than ever, she was convinced these same, vile men had murdered her Mr. Hutchinson.

She and Hannah shared the crowded coach with the four masked men. The ladies had been thrust to the floor, and their captors took the seats and rested their muddy boots (with no effort to be careful) on the ladies. The stench of the dirty cloth around her mouth caused her already-sickened stomach to roil even more.

It was impossible for Lucy to see where they were going. She believed they were in Mayfair and then on an even busier street. If she was not mistaken, they were near the river.

After about twenty minutes of navigating through streets snarled with whinnying horses, hansom cabs, saddlehorses, and clanging coaches, the carriage stopped. One of the men got out and looked around. "Ain't no one here to observe what we're doing."

He reached into the coach and grabbed Lucy. "I'll take the skinny one." He hoisted her over his shoulder. A quick glance around told her they were in an alley behind a row of houses that terminated at the river. He strode through the home's back door which led to a kitchen and scullery, but he went straight for the stairs.

When they reached the top of the stairs, she recognized the house. It was Count von Gustafsen's! No sooner had she discovered that than the count himself joined them. His gaze circled the chamber where the four henchmen and their two captives now stood. Then his cold blue eyes locked with hers. "You can remove the gag from the smaller woman."

"I demand to be released," she shrieked as soon as the cloth was removed.

The count gave a sinister laugh. "Ah, but you, Miss Beresford, will be the bait to snare Lord Montague."

Lord Montague? Her first thought was that his lordship was the target of the assassination. Then she thought not. "I assure you, I am of no consequence to Lord Montague."

"If you believe that, you're blind. I've seen the way he looks at you." He chuckled, a laugh without mirth. "Besides, I saw the way he held you in his arms that day at the park. He'll come."

She shook her head. "It's not at all what you think. He's merely looking out for me until Mr. Hutchinson . . . oh, my God, you killed my fiancé, didn't you?"

He looked at the foul men who'd captured her and Hannah. "A Swedish nobleman does not dirty his hands on such a deed. But it might interest you to know that while I was cultivating the friendship of London's *ton*, I was also combing the city's underworld to cull men like these who could do my dirty work for me."

"I suppose you had something to do with getting us out of London, sending us to Bath on the false hopes of finding Mr. Hutchinson."

He smirked. "You're most intuitive, Miss Beresford. You see, when I orchestrated that ploy, your Mr. Hutchinson was still alive, but it had come to my attention that Lord Montague was madly searching for his friend. It was imperative to me that before Hutchinson died, I had to know who else knew what he'd learned. I needed time. I had to get Montague away from London, out of my way and away from those who might hinder me if they knew of my plans. Now it looks as if I shall have to eliminate Lord Montague, too."

It felt as if her heart stopped. It was a moment before she could speak. She desperately needed to redirect his interest in murdering Lord Montague. "So you forged Mr. Hutchinson's hand to make us think he was in Bath?"

"I did." His gaze moved to the man who'd carried her here. "Take the women up to the attic."

The ropes at her ankles prevented her from walking. The count followed as she was being carried upstairs. She and a grumbling Hannah were taken to a small chamber lighted by a single candlestick held by the count. The room must have been a servant's bedchamber but which was now empty, save for a pair of wooden chairs.

A chill spiked through her when she saw its lone window had been boarded up.

"Since your Lord Montague knows about my cellar, I'll keep you here."

So his cook had told him about Lord Montague's excursion into the home's underbelly. Was that how the count had come to target his lordship? And her?

"Where did you take Mr. Hutchinson?"

"We kept him in the cellar." He gave that evil laugh. "Until my acquaintances here came and disposed of him. Poor man. He was so out of his element. He stupidly asked me outright if I were an assassin."

Her heart wept for the loss of her Reluctant Bridegroom. "Who do you plan to assassinate?"

"The Duke of Wellington. The pity of it is the man's never alone. I needed to befriend someone who could introduce me to the fellow, needed to get in the man's good graces. You see, I'm doing this for my good friend Napoleon. And once he reclaims his power, there will be no limit to my own power and wealth."

"How did your men dispose of my betrothed?" Saying those words hurt. Knowing she'd never again see Mr. Hutchinson hurt. Most of all, knowing she would soon be joining him terrified her.

"The word *cut-throat* aptly describes my assistants here. In the dark of night, they dumped his body into the Thames. They had taken the precaution of first rolling up his body and tying it in an old rug—along with a number of heavy bricks. Jim here used to be a sailor, and he knows how to tie knots that won't ever come undone."

"Why do you mean to harm Lord Montague?"

"Because I believe Thomas Hutchinson told him his suspicions about me."

"You're wrong. Lord Montague knows nothing. Mr. Hutchinson never told him anything. I will own, Lord Montague learned—after his friend went missing—about Mr. Hutchinson's mission, but Mr. Hutchinson had respected the clandestine nature of his assignment. Lord Montague was acting on his own, following up on a number of men he suspected of being the assassin. In fact, he believes Frenchmen are behind the plot."

"You'll forgive me if I don't believe you. You'd say anything to protect the man you've fallen in love with."

In that instant, she knew she had, indeed, fallen in love with Lord Montague. She would do anything to save his life. But what could she do, tied up in an attic? "I'm telling the truth."

The count eyed his henchmen. "Gag Miss Beresford once more."

The henchman who had carried her stood her on her feet to do as instructed, and Lucy tried once more to scream—joined by Hannah's muffled wails—in the hope that a neighbor might hear. The man reared back and slapped her with such force, the back of her head struck the wall. Blood trickled and splattered her dress as she crumbled into the nearby wood chair.

"Don't count on any of my servants coming to your rescue. They are loyal only to me. Besides, they're accustomed to my so-called dirty deeds."

She tossed a sympathetic look at Hannah and wished she could tell her how sorry she was that she had gotten her innocent maid into such mortal danger.

When the count and his candle left, the chamber was plunged into darkness.

<hr/>

MONTY HAD GONE home to exchange his coach for a saddlehorse. And to collect Cummings. Two could search better than one.

He had flown upstairs to his bedchamber where Cummings was pressing a cravat. "Miss Beresford and her maid are missing. We must find them. Fetch my sword. And pistol."

He could tell from the expression on Cummings' face, his valet was as worried about the maid as Monty was about Lucy. It was a good thing his valet knew how to use a pistol. "Arm yourself, too."

"It will be my pleasure, my lord, not that there's anything to be pleased about in this situation. I hope Miss Hannah's not been hurt."

"And I hope to God Lucy's unharmed."

The two men carried lanterns, and for hours they separately searched many of the paths that crisscrossed the park. It had grown beastly cold, and the wind was cutting through him, but he dismissed his own discomfort. His thoughts centered solely on saving the woman he loved.

It was well past midnight when he and Cummings met up again at the park's main gates. Both men were lower than an adder's belly. "How could two women just disappear from London's biggest park in broad daylight?" a dejected Cummings asked.

It suddenly occurred to Monty that Lucy may have tried to send for him. He must go to his house. Perhaps he'd find a note from her.

They raced to his Piccadilly mansion. On the sideboard in the home's entryway, Monty saw a piece of correspondence, and his hopes soared. He flew to it, but when he saw the handwriting, he knew that was not Lucy's neat little script. He tore open the missive and began to read.

> *If you wish to see Miss Beresford alive, you will come alone, unarmed, to St. Bartholomew's Chapel tonight.*

With trembling hands, he gave the letter to Cummings. "They've got the women."

Cummings scanned the letter. "It says you must come alone."

Monty nodded.

"I will not stand by and lose you or Miss Hannah," Cummings barked.

"We have no choice. I cannot do anything that will jeopardize Miss Beresford."

Chapter Twenty

STREETS HERE IN the City that normally bustled with the clopping and clanging of vehicles and raised voices and laughter had gone silent by this time of night. No squares of light spilled onto the dark street from the solid brick buildings Monty passed as he made his way along the dark and winding thoroughfare. He tightened his neck scarf to protect against the cold winds that slashed against him.

This journey would terminate in his death. Yet, even though he'd known Lucy for mere weeks, death was preferable to life without her—and without Hutch, who he knew now had to have met a murderous fate.

As his horse cantered along the Strand, Monty was powerless not to picture Lucy. The whitish blonde of her hair. The skin so fair that cold tinged it with blue. The soft rounding of her slenderness. He recalled the winsomeness of her youthful voice and the wisdom of her ideas. She might not be a classic beauty, but to him she was the most beautiful woman in the three kingdoms.

His heart softened when he remembered how wretchedly sick she'd become during their long carriage rides to and from Bath. Even then he'd been overwhelmed by the desire to protect her, to care for her, though he hadn't yet been able to admit it to himself.

She was so delicate, he worried about her even more now. A brute could crush her to death without even trying. The very thought unleashed a consuming rage within him. There was nothing he wouldn't do to protect her. Even if it meant giving up his life.

He passed the apex of the two streets which bounded St. Paul's Cathedral. Its towering gold dome shone in the moonlight. Moments later, he was once more in darkness as he turned onto the narrow lane where St. Bartholomew's Chapel was located. The skinny houses here obstructed any evidence of moonlight. He was only barely able to determine there were no horses, no conveyances, nor a single person on this lonely lane.

After a few moments, he came to the chapel. The cream-colored building stood out among the brick edifices surrounding it. He dismounted and secured his horse. As he approached the chapel's timbered double doors, his pulse accelerated, his hands sweat. He drew a deep breath, then eased open the door.

Inside, a lone lantern stood on the altar. Even before the door opened fully, two men—one from each side—pounced on him. The shorter grabbed his right arm, the taller man his left. It all happened so suddenly, Monty's latent efforts to resist failed. He should have been better prepared for the assault. Without any weapon, it would have been difficult for him to disable a pair of attackers, but he was still angry at himself for his complacency.

One of the ruffians yanked Monty's arms behind his back and tied them together with a length of rough hemp. The wiry little fellow possessed remarkable strength. The other, who was closer to Monty's size, stood in front of him, knife drawn and pointed directly at Monty's heart.

"Now to tie his mouth," the larger man instructed. "We can't have the gent squealing like a woman and calling attention to our . . . dealings."

Monty took exception to the comment. Not only would he never squeal like a woman, he would not have bellowed like a man, either. Not until he found Lucy. He wouldn't do anything that would prevent him from finding her.

"You don't have to do that," Monty said. "I came here of my own free will. I will come with you peacefully." The life of the woman they'd captured was too precious to him.

"You try anything, Jacob here will dig that knife of his into you."

Monty followed those dregs of humanity through the sacristy toward the chapel's rear door. He'd wager they'd never before seen the inside of a church. In the alley behind the chapel, another ill-dressed, ill-groomed man stood guard over a fine, unmarked coach. Upon seeing them, he swung open the coach door, and Monty climbed in, his two captors following.

Because there were few conveyances on the streets at this hour, they reached their destination in just a few moments. Monty recognized the house: Count von Gustafsen's.

Now he understood everything. Because of Monty's fiasco in the count's cellar, the Swede knew Monty was on the trail of his missing friend.

But how had he known the depth of Monty's feelings for his best friend's fiancée?

Even given the late hour, the fully dressed count greeted them as Monty and the miscreants entered the house. His eyes sparkled with malicious mirth. "I see I was right in my supposition regarding your affection for Miss Beresford."

I can't let him know how much I care. Monty chuckled. "You may not know about gentlemen, but as one, I must defend the lady in the absence of my closest friend, her betrothed."

"Come to my library. We must talk."

Like the other chambers in this house, the library's furnishings revealed decades—if not centuries—of wear. The count instructed his henchmen to stand guard outside the door.

"Since I shall be so heavily guarded, will you not untie my hands?"

The count eyed his captive and nodded.

As soon as the ropes were untied and the library door closed, the count said, "Do take a seat, my lord."

Both men chose high-backed armchairs near the smoldering fireplace. The count got straight to the point. "That you singled me out, that you attempted to search my house tells me that Mr. Hutchinson confided his suspicions to you. My inquiries inform me that you two men were exceedingly close and have been throughout your lives."

"You're dead wrong. Hutchinson told me nothing. Just think about it. Why would I have waited more than a week after he went missing to try to find him? You've killed him, have you not?"

"Of course. He was such an amateur. The poor fellow came right out and asked me if I was an assassin. What's an assassin to do?" He gave a vicious laugh.

Even though Monty had come to realize that Hutch had been murdered, its verification plunged him into a sudden, aching grief. A ravenous anger consumed him. If it weren't for Lucy, he'd kill this vile man with his bare hands without the slightest hesitation.

But Lucy's safety trumped everything. "What do you want from me?"

"It's imperative you tell me everything you know, that you tell me who knows what."

"You'll get no information from me until you release Miss Beresford."

The count yawned. "In that case, I shall ask you to sleep on it. My bed beckons." The count crossed the chamber, threw open the door and told his minions to take Monty to the attic.

When they reached the attic, Monty was shoved into a dark chamber. Its door was then slammed. The click of a lock sickened Monty.

Until he heard a muffled voice. *Lucy!* Though he couldn't discern words, her forlorn tone strummed on his heartstrings.

In spite of the total darkness, he rushed straight to her. Though he could not see, he thought she rose from a chair before pressing against him. He swaddled her in his passionate embrace. He caressed. He stroked. He murmured endearments. He pressed soft kisses into her rose-scented hair.

Last night's dream of holding her had left him euphoric and numb with want. But actually holding her in his arms dimmed last night's joy as starkly as lovemaking overshadowed handholding.

"Lucy?"

"Um huh?"

Those deviants had gagged her!

"Allow me to remove that wretched thing from your mouth."

Because of the complete darkness, it took a while before he could untie the double-tied knot on the filthy rag.

"Thank you, my lord," she said when he yanked it off.

"Arthur," he murmured. "Call me Arthur, my love."

She answered by standing on her toes and pressing her sweet lips against his cheek. A gift of the Crown Jewels could not have been as precious.

"Could you please untie my hands and feet?"

The ropes, too, were double knotted, but he soon freed her. She immediately pressed her slight frame into his, those slender arms closing round him, her sweet face nestled into his chest. "Thank you, m-m-my . . . Arthur."

In his hunger for her, he'd not thought to consider if his affections could be reciprocated. But now he knew.

Muffled, unintelligible sounds came from nearby. *The maid.*

Lucy drew a quivering breath and pulled away. "We need to untie Hannah," she said.

"Allow me." He was surprised his own voice was free of breathlessness.

As he set about removing the binds from Lucy's maid, he found himself wishing it were just the two of them—him and his precious Lucy—and he lamented the perilous situation that bound them all.

Yet, if Hutch had never gone missing, he would never have known Lucy as he did now, would never have known this consuming love.

"Blimey! That thing around my mouth be worse than having my hands tied behind my back," Hannah exclaimed into the darkness as soon as she was able to utter a word.

"It seems appropriate, Miss Hannah, to apprise you at this time of the fact Mr. Cummings was anxious on your behalf and would have come here himself to try to save you, but the instructions were explicit. I was to come alone and come unarmed if I cared about Miss Beresford."

The maid sighed. "And it is most obvious you do care for my mistress." Then Hannah squealed. "And Mr. Cummings must care for me! I ask you, is that not grand?"

"It would be quite grand were we to be permitted to leave this place," Lucy said, "but I must warn you, my dear, faithful Hannah, that is not likely to happen."

In his privileged life, Monty had never felt more impotent. All he could hope for was to be able to offer himself in exchange for the freedom of these two women.

"You mean I'll never see Mr. Cummings again?"

He hated to give these women false hope, so he remained silent.

"I cannot imagine a scenario that would free us from bondage," Lucy said, her voice solemn.

"I don't know what a scent-ario is."

He heard Lucy expel a long breath. "A scenario is sort of like a scene, but it's a scene which occurs only in one's imagination and it involves eventualities."

"There you go again with your fancy words. *Eventualities.*"

Lucy blew out another impatient breath. "And you should read more."

"You said I couldn't read yer newspaper no more because you didn't want me to read about them maniac killers." She let out a harrumph. "And here we be with maniac killers. If that ain't ironing."

"Irony," Lucy corrected sorrowfully, clasping Monty's hand tightly.

Before he could say anything of comfort, he must cause her pain.

He drew her tightly to him. "Hutch is dead."

"I know."

"As mournful as I am, my friend's death frees me to tell you what I've long wanted to. I have fallen in love with Miss Lucy Beresford. Totally and completely."

She pressed even closer to him. "I've felt so guilty for falling in love with you when my . . ." She stopped, her voice cracking. Sniff, sniff. "When I wasn't free to do so."

"I know, my love. I've felt the same."

His head lowered until his lips found hers, gently at first, then with a greater urgency. Her sweet tasting mouth opened to his. The pulsing of their mingled tongues nearly drove him mad with need.

He could almost die happy now that he possessed the love of the only woman who'd ever mattered to him. But more than ever, he wanted to live. Now that he'd found her, he wanted to lie beside her every night until his hair was white. He wanted to see her belly grow with the seed of his child. He wanted her as mistress of his homes. Most of all, he just wanted her. His Lucy.

He cupped her breast, his thumb smoothing over her erect nipple in slow circles until a wave of whimpers wracked her body and he remembered that, though the darkness was complete, they were not alone. Reluctantly, he pulled away.

"I don't suppose there's any way out of this chamber," Monty finally had the presence of mind to ask.

"There's a boarded-up window, but even were it not boarded, from this attic it would be a two-story drop to the ground," Lucy said.

"And as you probably could tell, the door's got a padlock on it," Hannah offered.

What of inside hinges? He raced as quickly as he dared to the door and began to feel. He went up the right side and down the left. No hinges. The count must have learned from Monty's earlier debacle.

"Since there's nothing we can do, you ladies may as well get some sleep. If nothing else, it will keep your mind off the peril." Monty settled a possessive hand at Lucy's waist and they moved toward the wall where she'd been standing when they'd kissed.

They dropped to the floor, and he kept his arm around her, pulling her close. The side of her face pillowed just beneath his shoulders. A cacophony of conflicting emotions surged through him. Sorrow. Bliss. Regret. Most of all, love. If only he had met her and fallen in love with her the year she came out. They could have had six long years together. She could have been his Lady Montague.

But that would never have happened. His arrogant self would have ignored the debutante who looked as if she still belonged in a schoolroom. He had Hutch to thank for bringing Lucy into his life. Hutch had been wholly unworthy of her—not that Monty was.

Perhaps his punishment for his arrogance was the torture of loving her and not being able to possess her. He was not such a fool that he believed he would ever walk out of this house. He just hoped to God Lucy could.

He stayed awake long after Lucy's steady breathing told him she was asleep. How he longed to share more nights with her. If only there was some way he could extricate them from captivity and flee to safety. It was a very long shot, but he would have to try to overpower the other men. When the women awakened, he would instruct them on the best way they could disable their captors: a knee thrust to the groin.

While his mind was churning with various scenarios of escape, he heard metal scraping the lock. It couldn't possibly be daylight yet. Surely the count needed more than an hour or two of sleep.

Why was it taking so long for his captors to open the lock? It was at least two minutes before the sounds stopped and the door opened.

There, bathed in light from the corridor, stood Cummings, dressed wholly in black.

Chapter Twenty-One

MONTY LEAPT UP, offered a hand to Lucy, who had been jolted awake, and spoke in a whisper. "By Jove! You're the best valet a fellow ever had!"

"Is Miss Makepiece unharmed?" Cummings asked, his voice hitched in worry.

Miss Makepiece? Who in the devil was that?

"Indeed I am!" Hannah shouted in far too loud a voice as she rushed to her rescuer.

"Quick!" Monty instructed, snatching Lucy's hand. "We've got to get out of here."

Keeping his voice low, Cummings said, "I've taken the liberty of bringing your lordship's sword and dagger."

Monty hurriedly started to strap on the sword, just as other doors on the same floor flew open. Three men in varying states of undress rushed into the corridor that was lighted from a single wall sconce. Hannah's exclamation must have awakened them. They'd not had time to arm themselves properly, but the tall one wielded a menacing-looking knife.

Unfortunately, the men stood between them and the stairway. Monty had to clear the way for the ladies. Sword in hand, he lunged at the lone armed man, attempting to strip him of the knife. The man with the knife retreated. Monty pursued. Terror flashed on the tall man's unshaven face. He whipped up his unwieldy knife in an attempt to dislodge Monty's rapier. Monty was quicker. He went for the man's gut, but the man's movement resulted in a mere grazing of his side as he moved farther back, farther away from Monty.

Though Monty couldn't see behind him, he was aware that Cummings, who was also armed, was keeping away the other two men.

Now Monty's opponent was cornered, his back against the wall. His terrified gaze flicked to the stairs he was dangerously close to. He was Monty's for the taking.

His gaze shifting from Monty to the steep stairway, he reared back his arm.

Monty's instincts kicked in as the knife came hurling toward his chest. He ducked and propelled forward. As he did so, his sword plunged into his enemy. The man's body careened down the stairs. He did, indeed, scream like a woman.

Another scream came from behind Monty. His gaze shifted. The knife the tall man had thrown at him arrowed right into his wiry little accomplice's back. Blood sprayed over him and pooled at his feet. No one could survive a wound so deep from a knife that huge.

As Monty pounded down the stairs, he heard Cummings ask the ladies for rope. After all the ruckus, silence was no longer necessary. At the landing on the floor below the attic, Monty knelt beside his assailant's lifeless body and felt for a pulse. The sword wound could not have been fatal, but the apparently broken neck was. It gave Monty no pleasure to realize the man was dead. Another death to lay at Count von Gustafsen's feet.

As Monty moved to stand up, something pricked his back. *The count.* He'd heard nothing. His pulse exploding, his grip on his sword tightening, Monty sprang to his feet and spun around to face Count von Gustafsen.

Dressed in a night shirt, the count leveled his sword at Monty's midsection. "I really don't want you dead, my lord. Not yet, anyway.

You possess information I need."

"You'll not need information where you're going. England hangs traitors." The two men were separated only by the length of their swords. "I propose we settle this like gentlemen. Let us begin at three paces." Monty did not trust the count to conduct himself as a gentleman. Surprisingly, the count obliged, giving Monty space to move to the center of the landing to mark off the paces. Never removing his gaze from the menacing Swede, Monty stepped back. *One.*

Each man stepped back three paces.

With more than ten feet between them now and no room to roam on the narrow landing with stairs ascending and descending at right angles on either end, Monty knew he did not want to have to defend himself while climbing the stairs backward toward the attic. He must act first.

"*En garde!*" Monty directed as he lunged forward.

The count proved to be gifted with the sword. The Swede's strength lay in his superior defensive skills. He was able to deflect each of Monty's thrusts. He was also surprisingly light on his feet. Somehow, he was managing to back Monty up. They came closer and closer to the dead body at the bottom of the attic stairs. Desperate to change the direction, to back the count up, Monty risked a fatal wound by charging toward the count.

Monty deflected the count's rapier. He then unmercifully drove the count back toward the other stairway, the one that went down. If he could get the count there . . . perhaps the vile man could meet the same fate as his minion had moments earlier.

Monty had never fought harder, his sword never quicker. Sweat covered him from head to waist as he forced the tiring count back to the opposite wall. The one at the top of the stairs.

When the count reached the wall, his face creased with panic. Then he reached back and hurled his sword at Monty. There wasn't room on the narrow landing for Monty to move out of the way.

Searing pain flared from Monty's side. Cursing, he yanked the sword's tip from his flesh, then tossed it over the balustrade. It clanged on the marble floors below.

Never removing his gaze from his opponent, Monty moved to the count. "I'll have you arrested for murder and treason."

The count gave a bitter laugh. "I prefer to go out on my own terms." He turned to the stairs and flung himself down.

Monty raced downstairs after him.

The count's body had stopped two steps away from the home's front door, one thin leg lodged—and snapped—between the banister posts. Blood streamed from his injured head.

Light from a pair of wall sconces shone on his lifeless face. Still holding his sword, Monty came to stand over the count. The man was not breathing.

"Arthur! You're hurt!"

He looked up to see Lucy as she raced down the stairs.

※

LUCY TOSSED HANNAH the rope Monty had removed from her. She had no time to assist Mr. Cummings in tying up the captor-turned-captive. Monty was in danger! From the attic's narrow corridor, she had watched in terror as Monty battled that evil count, fearing with every shaking breath this man she loved would be killed.

She was powerless to help. "Please hurry," she said to her lover's valet without peering in his direction. She prayed that as long as she was watching him, nothing bad could happen to Monty. "My lord needs help."

When the count's sword slashed into Monty, a shrill cry ripped from her lungs. She pounded down the stairs. Before she even reached the man she adored, she knew he was no longer in danger. The vicious count was dead.

And, thank God, her Monty was still standing!

A splotch of blood stained his coat. "We must call for a surgeon!" she cried.

He shook his head. "I'm all right. It's but a surface wound."

"Allow me to be the judge of that, my lord."

"Arthur."

She moved to him. "I beg that you remove your coat and shirt, my . . . my Arthur. Your life is very important to me." Just calling him *my Arthur* infused her with a heady sense of possession.

A grin pinching his handsome face, he stepped forward and drew her into his arms.

With bent forefinger, he lifted her chin, and lowered his head to tenderly kiss her. "You truly do want to remove my clothing here and now, Miss Beresford?"

She could only barely stop herself from joyful laughter. "Only your top clothing." She turned back to the valet, who was coming down the stairs. "Mr. Cummings, you and I shall see to your master's wound."

The valet rushed to the earl and immediately adopted a commanding stature as he began to remove his master's coat. Monty winced, peering at the blood oozing from the slit in his side. "It doesn't signify."

"We shall have to see for ourselves," Mr. Cummings said.

The valet then removed his employer's shirt. This time, it was the valet who winced. "That's a nasty-looking injury, my lord."

At the sight of blood trickling from his side, Lucy closed her eyes. It was too painful for her to look.

The valet took charge. "Allow me to probe, my lord."

She feared Monty might bleed to death. Still, she couldn't look. She could scarcely draw breath as she awaited the valet's pronouncement. Her queasiness matched what she experienced during long-distance coach travel, but now it was accompanied by an uncontrollable trembling.

She tried to tell herself that he was fine. He could talk. He could joke. He could kiss. Surely, he would not become another death attributed to the wicked count.

"I do believe you're right, my lord," Mr. Cummings finally said. "The wound's not deep, but we must stanch the flow of blood." He looked up and eyed Hannah, who'd come to join the others. "Pray, Miss Makepiece, could you look around and procure a length of some kind of clean cloth with which to bind his lordship?"

Hannah offered the valet an enthusiastic smile. "I know I'll find something in the kitchen." She stepped over the count's lifeless body and went toward the basement. A moment later she triumphantly returned and held up two squares of clean muslin.

Now that she was relatively assured her Monty wasn't going to die, Lucy watched as his servant tightly wrapped the wound.

When he finished, Monty came to Lucy, taking both her hands in his. "So you said my life was very important to you."

She was embarrassed to admit how thoroughly she adored this man. All she could do was nod.

He spoke in a low voice. "I believe we'll deal very well together. Will you spend your life with me? In my bed? As my Lady Montague? If you don't consent, I may have to throw myself down those stairs," he said with levity.

She felt as if she were in a dream, a dream where one's fondest desires were granted. It still seemed incomprehensible that a man as fine as the Earl of Montague could possibly fall in love with her, but she believed it to be so. "In that case, I shall have to oblige you and say *yes*."

Her arms came tightly around him.

With their servants both standing there, it was not a particularly private moment. Monty eyed his man. "Cummings, will you be the first to offer felicitations upon my upcoming nuptials?"

"Indeed, my lord. This is wondrous news." Cummings' gaze

flicked to Hannah, then back to his employer. "I suppose this means Miss Makepiece and I shall be residing under the same roof?"

"Indeed it does, my good man. For now, though, I have a commission for you. Since the sun has now risen, I shall draft a letter explaining this night's activities, and you shall deliver it to Lord Stewart. He'll need to send soldiers to collect these . . . men."

Monty then turned back to Lucy. "But first, I must kiss my beloved Chameleon."

Epilogue

WITH PUMPKIN PURRING loudly on her lap and Hannah putting the finishing touches on her hair, Lucy watched her maid in the looking glass.

"'Tis a pity your cousins won't be here for your wedding. Just think, I am to be maid to a real lady! *Lady Montague*. And Mr. Cummings and I will . . . well, that remains to aspire."

"*Transpire*. I believe, my dear Hannah, you and your Mr. Cummings will also marry."

The maid's eyes widened. "You would permit that, my lady?"

"You cannot address me as *my lady* until tomorrow. And, yes, of course I'd permit you to marry. Your happiness is very important to me, and I believe dear Monty is desirous of fulfilling his valet's wishes. They're very close."

When Hannah set down the brush and proclaimed Lucy's hair perfection, Lucy kissed the top of the cat's head and set him down. She stood and sighed. "How I wish my cousin Harriett could be here for my wedding."

"Brighton ain't that far away. Why do you not just send for her?"

"A subject does not interfere with the Regent's plans."

"Yer just as important as yer fancy Lady Harriett. After all, you're to become the wife of an earl. Her husband's a mere baronet."

"She saved the Regent's life."

"And you saved the Duke of Wellington's! I read all about it in this morning's newspaper. And, besides, the duke's much more popular than that fat Regent."

A tapping at her chamber door was followed by Judson announcing that Lord Montague awaited her in the library.

Unable to suppress a smile, she raced down the stairs to the library. No longer was her future husband relegated to the stuffy drawing room. These past two days they had met in the intimate library, the room where his smoldering attentions had first signaled that he might just be attracted to her. They had come to think of it as *their* library, even though her cousin Devere's influence permeated the chamber.

She went straight into his arms, and they kissed. "I've procured the special license."

It was still difficult to believe that tomorrow this wonderful man would become her husband. Could anyone be happier than she was? "I cannot wait."

He stole one more kiss, this one much hungrier than the last.

As much as she was enjoying it, they needed to talk. She pulled back slightly, her eyes meeting his. "Have you seen the morning papers?"

He nodded. "My affianced is a celebrity."

"I was very sad. There was no mention of poor Mr. Hutchinson. He's the real hero. He gave his life to his country."

"You're right. He was a hero," Monty said solemnly. "I'll talk to Lord Stewart about that, make sure there's an article about our deceased friend. Maybe they will even erect a statue of him or give him some other honor befitting his sacrifice."

"He certainly deserves it." She looked up into Monty's dark eyes. "Though I couldn't have married him, you know."

"Were you in love with him?"

She thought about her response for a moment. "I may have fancied myself in love some years ago, but his neglect destroyed that. And when I met you, I began to understand what real love was."

Just as he was about to kiss her again, the library door flew open.

And there stood Devere, a lovely woman beside him, Lady Harriett next to her, and a man Lucy presumed to be Lord Rockingham.

Harriett spoke first. "You've eclipsed my fame, Lucy! I'm so proud of you."

"I wouldn't be here were it not for Lord Montague," Lucy responded.

Devere's gaze shifted to Monty. He barely nodded and said, "Your servant, Lord Montague."

Monty strode to her cousin, the head of the Beresford family. "I hope you don't object, but I plan to wed your cousin, Miss Beresford, tomorrow."

Harriett shrieked. "Oh, Lucy! I am so happy you're not marrying that horrid Thomas Hutchinson. Do say you'll have me as your witness."

"Nothing could please me more, but I must tell you that evil Count Gustafsen killed poor Mr. Hutchinson. My former fiancé was a true hero—even if he did treat me abominably."

Devere offered Monty a solid handshake. "We're delighted to welcome you to the family, my lord." Then he cast a glance at Lord Rockingham. "You know my new brother-in-law Lord Rockingham, do you not?"

"Indeed I do. I've long admired his Parliamentary accomplishments."

"How nice to have another Whig in the family," Devere said.

Harriett sidled up to her bridegroom. "I must make you known to my husband, dear Lucy."

Introductions were made all around.

Devere called for champagne to be served, and when it came, he toasted the betrothed couple first, then he said, "I do pray there will be no more dangerous adventures in the Beresford family."

The three couples, each holding hands and clasping the stems of their glasses, enthusiastically agreed with the Earl of Devere.

About the Author

Since her first book was published to acclaim in 1998, Cheryl Bolen has written more than three dozen Regency-set historical romances. Several of her books have won Best Historical awards, and she's a *New York Times* and *USA Today* bestseller as well as an Amazon All Star whose books have been translated into nine languages. She's also been penning articles about Regency England and giving workshops on the era for more than twenty years.

In previous lives, she was a journalist and an English teacher. She's married to a recently retired college professor, and they're the parents of two grown sons, both of whom she says are brilliant and handsome! All four Bolens (and their new daughter-in-law) love to travel to England, and Cheryl loves college football and basketball and adores reading letters and diaries penned by long-dead Englishwomen.

Check out these sites of hers:
subscribe to newsletter – littl.ink/newsletter
blog – blogl.ink/RegencyRamblings
website – www.CherylBolen.com
facebook – fbl.ink/Facebook
Pinterest – littl.ink/Pinterest
Readers' group – facebook.com/groups/2586590498319473

Made in the USA
Las Vegas, NV
26 April 2024

89168734R00108